C000139758

Born to a Greek mother and a Scottish father in the cultural town of Paisley, in the west of Scotland on October 24th 1989. Mr Morris was exposed to a fantastical range of mythical cultures from an early age, stemming from both Grecian and Caledonian backgrounds.

Ever since the age of eight, Chris had begun to create a whole world of magic and mythology within his mind which he then used as a means of role play with his friends. And so, for many years, Chris had continued to tell the stories of his world along with his buddies, until they were too old to continue playing imaginary.

But that didn't stop Chris from wanting to keep his world and characters alive, and so he took to literature where he began to write in-depth backgrounds to all of his characters and that of his world which he prides as his greatest achievement.

The journey to Piathos, however, was not an easy one as Mr Morris struggled with many obstacles, including Tourette syndrome, non-epileptic seizures and dyscalculia, which landed him within a school for special needs.

But with a sharp mind and determination, Chris wanted to learn more and thus he pushed himself into further education, all the while joining with the town's local writers group before commencing into college where he began to write the first in series *Warriors of Piathos: The Circle of Destiny* all the while studying Media at Cardonald Campus.

Chris then decided to choose the pen name Chrys K. M. to honour his mother's maiden name Chrysostomou, his old nickname as a child, Kazama. And his father's surname Morris. Chris is now also a member of Paisley's up-and-coming comic bookstore Comicrazy where he partakes in a lot of Dungeons and Dragons and runs an open-world campaign of the exciting and expanding universe of Piathos.

I would like to dedicate this book to my supportive and coaching father, Andrew. My late and proud mother, Dora. All my crazy and amazing friends at Comicrazy, and the sword and shield, my fantastic agent and good friend, Stephen Magill, who stood by me throughout all of the highs and lows for the past five years.

To Aimaa

Discaur your pours
from Pistons to Earth

[signature]

Chrys K. M.

WARRIORS OF PIATHOS: THE CIRCLE OF DESTINY

AUSTIN MACAULEY PUBLISHERS™

LONDON • CAMBRIDGE • NEW YORK • SHARJAH

Copyright © Chrys K. M. (2019)

The right of Chrys K. M. to be identified as author of this work has been asserted by him in accordance with section 77 and 78 of the Copyright, Designs and Patents Act 1988.

All rights reserved. No part of this publication may be reproduced, stored in a retrieval system, or transmitted in any form or by any means, electronic, mechanical, photocopying, recording, or otherwise, without the prior permission of the publishers.

Any person who commits any unauthorised act in relation to this publication may be liable to criminal prosecution and civil claims for damages.

A CIP catalogue record for this title is available from the British Library.

ISBN 9781528912693 (Paperback)
ISBN 9781528960212 (ePub e-book)

www.austinmacauley.com

First Published (2019)
Austin Macauley Publishers Ltd
25 Canada Square
Canary Wharf
London
E14 5LQ

Thanks to all of my championing friends at Comicrazy (Scott, Callum, Corbin, Andrew, Gilbert, Alex, Jamie and the owner John.)

Thanks to my beloved family and friends (Jeanne, my dad Andrew, Piper, Martin, Jack, Adam, Isaac, Daniel, Daryl, David, Higgins, Gregor, Lee and many more…)

And a special thanks to my good friend, the first person to take my dream seriously when not many did. The reason I have been able to work so hard and make everyone else proud. My sword and shield… My agent, Stephen Magill.

I would also love to give a special mention to my beautiful late grandmother, Nana Wanda; may she rest upon easy tides.

A Time Before Destiny

Chapter 1
In the Beginning

Return the hands within the clock,
reverse the face of time
rewind it back from whence it came,
erase it all from history's mind.

Water, land, day and night is a constant cycle of life. As the very first breath was endured in the blue of the sea, it compelled itself to be next drawn on land. Spinning an eternal wheel of light and dark, the sun and the moon brought order to the lands near and far, turning from the face of Earth and to the many other worlds of far and beyond.

Piathos was the first living planet and the very birth place where the seeds for all worlds were grown before being sprinkled out into the heavens, where they would eventually expand and circle the magnificent stars.

Guarding the mystical temple, which brought life to the cosmos, were the four Oracles of Piathos. Black, the eldest sister, harboured the powers of night and protected all within its nocturnal domain. White, the second eldest sister, commanded day and nurtured all that walked within its light; while the third sister, Blue, ruled over the seas and stood watch over all that dwelled within the deep. And finally, there was the youngest sister, Green, who stood as a sentinel for all within the land and the skies.

Piathos was home to many spectacular creatures and the origin of where magic was born. Warrior merfolk expanded into the oceans, forming the planet's tribal people. Elves and fairies were scattered between the mountain ranges, far lands and the forests where they would eventually become known as the land clans. And finally, the Dragons took to the skies as well as the canyons and caves of the world and because of their great intelligence, they soon came to be known as the wisdom of Piathos. And so, the Oracles watched over their world, secondary to their great and mighty King, Andreas Feather.

King Andreas was just and true, his mighty power unmatched by any mortal being beneath him. He was, in fact, an Archangel, who was sent from the Celestial realm to ensure that the will of Eternia, the universal force of good could be nurtured safely by his own creation, the Oracles of Piathos.

But before the reign of the great and wondrous King, there was a dark force which was brutally cold and uncompassionate. The dark brother of Eternia, jealous of the kinship and unity that Piathos had fostered, Zealous the dark entity of The Nothing, slowly began to shed his emptiness over the great and wonderful planet, causing fear and dread to soar across the land in an unforgiving wave of chilling hollowness.

But in response, King Andreas of the City of Angels raised his defences and entombed The Nothing deep within the crevasses underneath his castle grounds...

"Never again is Zealous to roam free," were the words spoken by the King.

Trapped in a constant loop of repetitive time, The Nothing lingered for centuries, all alone in the darkness. Unable to feed from any life force to give him sustenance, over time, it became weaker and humbled to Andreas' spell.

But, forever in time was not to be his fate, for Zealous was still part of Eternia, and one simply could not outweigh the existence of the other.

Chapter 2
The Oracle Sisters

'Return the hands within the clock,
reverse the face of time.
Rewind it back from whence it came,
erase it all from history's mind'

Black muttered to herself while sitting on her dark, silken bedsheets within the Temple of the Oracles.

She gazed out at the world from her chamber, as the coral star began to rise and dawn broke free. As glowing daylight started emanating from one corner of the Kingdom to the next, all walks of life living under White's rule suddenly began to blossom into wakefulness.

"What is that, Black? It may not be night yet, dear sister. For my light has but only just begun to shine through the darkness," stated her sister White, as she too glanced out at the beautiful, amber sky which was slowly beginning to turn blue. This sight could not however compare to the pair of woman that stood watching it.

Black was extremely beautiful to gaze upon. A real night vision as it were, her twilight-blue eyes and long, silken, black hair glided out behind her as she turned. Her milky-white skin beamed radiantly, like the full moon on a hot summer night. Her long, navy-blue-black dress resembled that of the vastly extended night sky, with diamonds so dazzling that they appeared to favour the ever-sparkling and distant stars.

White, too, was an exquisite radiance to behold, with her long, white blonde hair that danced alongside her in the fresh morning breeze. Her spring-green eyes sparkled like dazzling emeralds when exposed to the light of day and her long, golden-white frock too was a sight to see, as it radiated warmth and comfort with each pattern and design that glistened through the fabrics. Each weave of her dress was made of Piolan gems that glowed like the cosmos at dawn, whenever she stepped into the light.

Black turned to her sister and smiled lovingly upon her.

"Not at all, my dear, I was just reciting the enchantment that our great King and maker, Andreas, once used to bring peace to this land."

White returned the smile as she extended out her hand and asked, "May we walk together, dear sister?"

"Yes, I think we may," Black chuckled, as she accepted her sister's hand. "Let us go and find our other sisters."

***

The two eldest Oracles emerged from their dazzling stone home, walking down to the beach that skirted the temple. As they approached the sand, looking for Blue, they suddenly happened upon a wounded mermaid that was bleeding heavily across the sea bay.

"What has happened here?" White asked sternly as she heard the cries of the injured tribeswoman.

As the sisters approached the injured soldier just outside of their home, the mermaid suddenly became assertively defensive, hissing and spitting.

As the Oracles grew closer, she snarled and bared her sharp teeth, her tailfin spikes pointed at the sisters. The mermaids of Piathos were usually more peaceful and never climbed ashore to hunt as their horizontal fins were not hard enough to endure the land; unlike the mermen, who had vertical fins that were razor-sharp and useful for climbing trees if land hunting was required.

Black and White gazed upon the mermaid with concern as they both raised their hands to show they meant no harm. "What has happened here?" Black asked while slowly stepping toward the injured seawoman.

The mermaid hissed again, shouting, "Stay back witch…!"

"Sister, something has bitten her," White said, "look at the teeth marks embedded in her tail."

Black then gazed at the wound and saw that the mermaid was bleeding out rapidly. As she extended her hand to offer her help, a strange and ominous shadow slithered below the water's surface.

"Sister, look there!" White exclaimed as a giant, black sea-monster with glowing yellow eye emerged from the watery depths.

"The Eel," the mermaid growled as she plucked a snake skeleton arrow from her quiver and placed it finely onto the string of her bow.

"Close your eyes, dear sister," White spoke as she lunged forward to protect the injured and beached mermaid. Just as the giant eel monster leaped high into the air above them, White waved her arms as she confidently cast her spell.

'O' light, le pen don soler.'

Suddenly, there was a massive blast of sunlight that emitted from the skies above and around the daylight sister. She then focused her energy forward in a stunning burst of power which burned and blinded the ginormous monstrosity, sending it plunging back into the water.

Back into the depths of the sea, the blinded and deeply wounded creature slithered down below the surface, where it vanished from sight.

Just then, a whirlpool of water emerged onto land and from its twirling vortex stood the third Oracle sister, Blue.

"Sister White, we must go to the Kingdom of Angels at once," Blue spoke while attending to her mermaid's wounds.

"There you go, Rathaka. I have sealed over your wounds with my magic. Now if you could return to your tribe and let Titanium know that I shall be down in due time to discuss these matters with him more thoroughly, I would be much obliged," the third Oracle stated, as she turned back to her sisters.

Blue was also something of dear and divine beauty. Her long, ginger and turquoise, mermaid-like hair billowed out in the ocean breeze as her deep-blue eyes reflected the ever-changing tides. Her frock, however, was more plated in shining oceanic armour unlike her older sisters who both harboured a more quaint and elegant attire of jewels and stones.

"Is it what we have foreseen, dear Blue?" White asked, as the mermaid dove away, now cured of her wounds.

"Yes, I fear it is, dear sister," Blue muttered as Black gazed at them with a confounded expression. "Our father fears that his spell weakens with every passing moment and that these beings that are occurring are only just the beginning of Zealous returning."

"What do you speak of with such trepidation, my sisters?" Black asked as she intervened into the subject which she had been previously privy to.

White turned to Black and smiled sadly as she caressed her sister's face with her hand and spoke softly, "My dear sister, it is not for me to tell you. I am sorry. Father will make everything clear in due time."

And then within moments, both Blue and White had vanished from the sea bay in a beam of joyous sunlight and a whirling vortex of water, leaving Black alone and confused, wondering what was transpiring behind her back, as she stood idle by the calm of the sea shore.

Chapter 3
Council at the Kingdom of Angels

"This is what I have feared for many hundreds of years," King Andreas addressed to his court, his voice echoing out even before the words left his mouth.

"My spell is losing its strength, and with every passing moment, the seal that binds The Nothing to his prison weakens further," the ten-feet-tall Celestial spoke.

King Andreas was an image not to be trifled with. He stood at ten-feet-tall, with muscles that had muscles. Strapped to his side was one of the most glorious of Celestial Artefacts, the Archean Sword. His stunning, long, white beard and hair billowed out in the most delicate wisp as he walked around the centre of his court which was circular in equal form. Andreas' fierce yet truthful, sharp, white-blue eyes cut through any soul that ever dared to unjustly oppose his laws.

Eclipse, the keeper of the Dragons, Lunar Mystic and chief of his people within the higher council of the City of Angels, stepped forward to speak.

"Our days of peace are but numbered, your majesty. For I have foreseen the malicious forces of Zealous befall all within this land. And so Zealous will return from the prison of time that you, my King, have so masterfully crafted," the slender elf flattered.

Eclipse was a tall, slender figure and was known to the court as one of the most loyal of soldiers within the council. Though despite his great reputation, King Andreas always felt that there was something odd about the Lunar Mystic and his devotion to the realm.

King Andreas then raised his hand to the white-blue-skinned elf that was standing before him dressed in his silken red robes.

"Before The All wound the hands of time and before he spun the threads of life, there was nothing. No light, no dark, nothing. I know exactly what you're going to say, Eclipse, about how the entities are of the same cloth."

"Ah, but of course, your majesty, you see, the Nothing was also there at the beginning. Two minds, two personalities, two brothers, but yet they are of the same cloth," Eclipse spoke as his long, dark hair glistened in the light that was filtering through the stained-glass windows of Andreas' home.

"Silence…!" Andreas yelled, his eyes flashing. "Do not believe that you that can speak of the gravity of this situation! Yes, the entities are of kin, but knowledge of the old belongs within the Book of Ancients, a book which no one is allowed to read. And we council today to speak of the uprising of evil and the history of that evil, I do not need to be lectured by you of it!"

All members of the council became silent from the echo of his great voice as it reverberated around the walls inside his court, forcing Eclipse to lower his head and silently retreat back into the crowd.

"Time is what can be used to defeat an entity such as The Nothing. Naught else that we, the elders of the land, have could be enough to quell it. Our power will only feed its never-ending appetite," Andreas continued, "although there is, however, one other option in fighting The Nothing… My first creation… Black, but this would be at the risk of her life and more importantly her soul. She is dear to me however, and I cannot bring myself to let her know even now."

This surprising revelation caused indistinct chatter to begin amongst the council members. Just then, another elder of the city stepped forward and raised her hands so that she might be heard. She was a tall and slim female elf that was wearing a green robe to indicate that she was the leader of the wood elf community. Her eyes were aluminous green and her hair was a verdant wash which blossomed with flowers as she stepped forward into the circle. Her hair was scented with perfume so potent that it eased the crowd from their tensions and stress.

"Great Royal Highness, I, Woodflower, of the forest people serve under Green, one of your four Oracles. We live harmoniously beside the great sea tribes of this land. There has been great dispute amongst the merpeople, and many battles have already begun to wage forth for the territory of sanctuary below the ocean waves. Many dark and dangerous monsters only spoken of in fables have suddenly begun to emerge from the shadows of the deep to ascend upon us the utmost horror."

Eclipse then raised his hands again so that he could interject on the wood elf's council. "The tribe folk of the ocean battle all the time, this is nothing peculiar," he said.

"Silence, Eclipse, let her speak," Andreas spoke evenly, the danger apparent in his voice, his authority charging through the mystic like thunder and lightning.

Woodflower again humbled herself to the great King before continuing forth with her statement, "Sire, I have never seen such carnage in the sea. There have been countless attacks on the Tiger Shark Tribe by monstrous Eel that were only ever spoken of in stories and legend."

Andreas gave an expression of concern as he continued to listen to Woodflower's statement.

"Sire, these Eels…they are not normal. They are monstrous and bigger than anything that I have ever seen. Their faces… they are…" the horror of their image haunted her as she spoke.

"They move so swiftly and deadly. I cannot begin to imagine the havoc that they wreak amongst the sea tribes."

Nodding his head in agreement, Andreas rose from his throne and kneeled beside the elf.

"I have heard. These beasts do not belong in our oceans," he whispered before rising from her side and addressing his fellow elders, "thank you for your council. I will take into consideration the matters that you have all brought to me."

Smiling up at the King, Woodflower gave one final curtsey before returning to the circle of the elders in the crowd.

Taking the centre of the room once again, Andreas sharply addressed his elders a message of concern and warning, "Once my time loop breaks, The Nothing will be free and its forces will once again reign upon my Kingdom. Go forth and prepare your kin, for I will need strong allies if we are to ride out this coming wave of hollow darkness."

Standing forward again, Eclipse signalled to the King and interjected with a question so sensitive that it shocked the Celestial to even think upon it.

"Sire, what of the other...defence that we have which stands against the power of Zealous?"

Despite the shock of Eclipse's dreaded question, Andreas swiftly and confidently returned to his throne and sighed.

"Unlike anything else, there is but one power aside from a loop which can starve Zealous into being humbled once again," the King spoke, "The Nothing is always feeding and always growing. Although the power of absolute darkness can indeed suffocate even the eternal force which is the Nothing. Hence, my first creation is the perfect weapon. But if she becomes tainted by its touch, then she herself will become absolute darkness."

Just then, the doors to the throne room swung open, allowing the golden light of the coral star to bleed harmoniously into the great chamber. From the great doors of the throne room emerged three of Andreas' Piolan Oracles, White, Blue and Green.

The youngest Oracle, Green, stood idle by her two older sisters as they entered gracefully into the great hall. She was absolutely adorable with her appearance like that of a princess of a woodland fairy tale. Her long, wavy, brown-and-green curls danced alongside her as she walked in motion with her siblings. Her milky-white skin almost glittered in the daylight as did her jade-green eyes which sparkled like the stained-glass windows of her King's castle in the sun. Her frilly, silken gown was laced beautifully with the gentlest looking of pink blossoms, though vines and thorns also graced her divine and softer appearance.

"My daughters, welcome," Andreas smiled proudly before turning to the members, "Council is dismissed, and elders are now free to leave and return to their lands."

"Father, there has been another attack," White said as she stepped through the motion of the bustling crowd, "and I fear that we cannot conceal your plan from Black any further. If she discovers the truth, then her noble act of heroism will only be to her own sacrifice. I cannot risk the thought of it and the terrible retribution that it would bring if she were to become absolute darkness."

"Come and dine with me, my daughters," Andreas muttered as the last of the city council members vanished from their view, "we haven't much time left, and I need to prepare myself for what is next to come."

Chapter 4
Answers Breed More Questions

Sitting alone in her chamber back at the Oracles Temple, Black began to ponder alone in silence as the light of day slowly passed by.

"Something isn't right. I just know it," she spoke aloud while falling into deeper thought.

Then, all of a sudden, something dawned upon her as she lay back on her silken, dark bedsheets. "The conversation at the bay..." she sighed, "hmm, I wonder?"

Mere moments later, an odd yet eerily compelling humming sound came from one side of her room. Black suddenly lunged forward, sitting atop her bed, gazing at what appeared to be a clear glowing orb of changing colours and light as it hovered just a few feet before her eyes.

"The Great Sight," she whispered while standing to her feet, "What is it you wish to show me, O' Celestial Artefact?"

The swirling orb of light then suddenly began to spring around in the air as it bounced and hopped along out of her chamber and up through the majestic hallways of the Oracles Temple. Black eagerly followed the dancing ball of light up into the tower because despite her family's secrecy, she knew that there was a bigger part for her to play.

Black continued to trail behind the glowing bubble that illuminated the shadowy stone coil of the tower's twirling stairwell. The higher she went the more she started to feel herself becoming hypnotised by its enchanting and Celestial magic.

Her eyes were fixed solidly onto the orb as it hovered and danced towards an altar, where it settled and became a solid ball of crystal which emanated its soft and heavenly light upon her skin.

Feeling warm and calm in its presence, the illuminated orb then let out another burst of rainbow light as it compelled the eldest Oracle to lay her hands atop its smooth and glassy surface...

"Show me..."

Her voice whispered hauntingly as she gazed longingly into the images that were forming before her.

***

"Father, father...! We haven't got much time left..." White's voice echoed through the crystal's glass as Black gazed down upon her family as they ate together at a long, golden dining table.

"You sense it too, don't you?" Andreas spoke, taking a silver chalice of dream-fruit wine in hand, "Eclipse. There is something very strange about him."

"Yes, father," White responded as she plucked a sweet pinkberry from her plate, "we cannot see Eclipse clearly when we use the Celestial Artefact for there is a strange mist that surrounds him."

At this point, White commenced eating, leaving Green to continue on.

"We believe that he is harnessing the power of Zealous through some kind of a Dark Artefact," Green said.

"Hmm, yes and he did seem very interested in what I had to say about Black," Andreas added, "if he is the traitor within my court, then he truly has his real intent shielded by the darkness that lingers below... Keep an open eye my children for he may come after your sister next."

Focusing more in depth to Andreas' words, Black turned her gaze to her father's face and studied him closely.

"Black may just very well be our only hope in this strife," he said, "though I fear that if she is exposed to The Nothing, then she would become an even greater threat than we face now."

Taken back by the sudden shock of it all, the stunned Oracle turned her baffled head towards her sisters and continued to gaze on in hopes for answers to the looming questions that were brewing in her mind.

"The Book of Ancients speaks of Artefacts so powerful that they could create beings of immortal status," Blue said while finishing off her plate of roasted Piolan seabird, "yet only the fair folk or the Sea Nymphs would harbour the magics so old to create such a powerful Artefact."

"The fair folk are under my command and protection," White stated firmly. "The Isle of the Sea Nymphs is an entirely different story, but I digress. If Eclipse is the traitor, then how do we find out what his true motives are?"

"We wait…" Andreas sighed before standing from his seat, "I will do all that I can to make sure that Black does not have to sacrifice herself. Return to me the Book of Ancients for I need to prepare my energies in beginning the Celestial time loop once again."

"Yes, father," White smiled as she, too, stood from her seat. "We will go forth and converse with the leaders of our own factions if we are in fact under any kind of threat."

"Be well," Andreas finished before his Piolan Oracles vanished from the dining table.

***

Returning from her vision within the Great Sight, Black recoils for a brief moment as she tries to register the scene to which she has just bore witness.

"I must go to the mystical Isle of the Sea Nymphs. If I am to indeed discover the truth that I hope to find…" she said to herself before taking in hand her long, black, hooded cloak and fleeing out of the Oracles Temple and escaping into the vast forest of the Piolan wilderness.

Chapter 5
Isle of the Sea Nymphs

And so, when the remaining three sisters returned to their temple to retrieve the Book of Ancients for their father, they noticed the lack of sound and the absence of their sister.

"Where is Black?" Green asked as she peered around at the tower peak before noticing that the door to the sacred room had been inwardly breached, "Why is the tower door open?"

White pondered to herself for a moment before turning her gaze to the shining, glassy surface of the Great Sight which reflected moonlight through its clear sphere.

"It has called to her. The Great Sight must have let her in," the blonde woman breathed.

Just then, the disturbing sound of crying and wailing could be heard emanating from the sea just beyond the Blue Caves of the Oracles Temple.

"My people," Blue gasped, "they need me!"

"Go to them!" Green encouraged.

Turning away from White and Green, Blue once again vaporised into a vortex of water, flew from the window and like a wave, curled herself into the foams of the deep vast sea outside the temple.

Green and White both gazed out of the giant stone window which faced directly above the Celestial Artefact and out to the open sea. Almost the entire tribe of the Tiger Shark folk had emerged to the surface where they met with their goddess Blue, the Oracle of the sea.

"Who did this?" Blue inquired as the chief of the Tiger Sharks slowly began to emerge from the waves. Water poured down from his horns and through his ginger hair and beard, as he pulled himself further upwards above the watery surface.

"Oracle of the sea, I heard news of a meeting with you, earlier today. But alas, we have been attacked by the opposing tribe of the Great Whites. Many have set themselves against us! I have called upon my brothering tribe to attend meetings about these raids, my lady," Titanium spoke as he whipped his razor-sharp fishtail back and forth within the shallows of the water.

"I think that the other tribes are fighting with you because of the Eel," Blue addressed firmly. "We must meet with their leader if we are to avoid more bloodshed."

"I, Titanium of the Tiger Sharks, must go forth into battle if we are to return our territory with honour," he responded, holding a similar tone.

Blue turned her gaze backwards to the temple where she spotted her two sisters gazing down upon them from the sacred room at the tower's peak.

"I will come with you now, and we will address this problem before it gets further out of my hands," the Oracle replied.

Becoming water once again, Blue then sank below the surface of the waves where she floated off under the currents like a glowing pulse of aquatic energy.

"We must go to the deep at once!" Titanium commanded as he signalled the legion of his guardsmen to turn their tails back and return to the depths of the coral below.

***

Meanwhile, as Black walked the clear path within the woodlands of the wood elves territory, she turned her blue-eyed gaze upon the mystical Isle of the notorious and ancient Sea Nymphs. The island stood idle and isolated in the foggy outlands between the Solar and Lunar Mystic mountains.

As Black reached the mysterious glowing isle that seemed to hover above the mountain clouds, she stepped forward towards the mysterious island which was glowing in the white aura of the Piolan moonlight. In front of her feet, lay an eerie and ominous pathway. Before her was a haunting, old, ropey, wooden bridge, and filled with conflicting emotions, Black decided to face her fears and step onto it.

She passed the old, wooden and ropey crossing until she stepped foot onto the ancient soil where the plants glowed hypnotically and the pollen wisped sweetly.

'Oracle of night, you truly have great power! The most potential we have ever seen...'

The echoing voice of a female spoke.

"Reveal yourself," the Oracle commanded as the images of dancing girls could be seen passing through the luminous glows of their alien plant life.

'Destined to become Black Poison, the goddess of the shadows will ascend into absolute darkness.'

The female voices spoke in echoing in waves of each other.

Black started moving around in a circular motion searching for whom and what it was that was taunting her.

"Reveal yourself!" Black called out strongly.

The voices chuckled playfully in the distance as they continued to dance and prance between the light and the shadows.

'We want to play with mother.'

One of the girls giggled.

'Yes, mother Blue, we want to play.'

"Enough games," Black grunted before raising her left arm and placing her hand over the glow of the Piolan full moonlight.

'O' shadow lio morbos Islumanti, luner.'

Suddenly, the entire isle became cloaked in a veil of shadowy energy which began to dull out the alien glows of the Sea Nymphs' lush and bright, fertile home.

'The Nothing will consume everything and twist morality into darkness! Black Poison is who you are destined to become. Once Zealous is free there will be a small window of opportunity to suffocate him. Act quickly before all that you know is consumed by absolute darkness'

The Sea Nymphs cried out hysterically before using their mystical energy to shove Black back across the wooden bridge that connected them to the outside world.

As soon as Black came to a halt on the other side of the rope bridge, a massive gust of wind blew from a crevasse below a nearby mountain, knocking Black off of her feet as the shadowy dome that circled the Sea Nymphs Isle dispersed and vanished into the ether, their home was aglow once again.

"Sister," Green exclaimed as she swirled into the forest in a vortex of wind, "I have come to watch and council my wood elf kin. Why is it that I find you lying on the ground within my court?"

Black smiled up at her youngest sister as she stood from the ground and dusted herself free of any twigs and forest debris.

"I too came into the forest to find council, dear sister."

As Green gazed back at Black with a glance of caution, the moonlight above shone down upon the isolated Isle of the Sea Nymphs in the distance, indicating that her presence there had just been seen.

"Did you really go to them, dear sister?" Green asked. "You know as well as I that they only answer kindly to Blue because of their aquatic similarities."

"I did, my sister," Black confessed, "but it is only because of what the Great Sight had showed to me that I felt compelled to seek further answers."

Green turned her gaze away from her sister, a look of guilt etched across her face. She knew that Black had made herself the target of her own fate. "Please sister, go home, you are no longer safe out here."

Black in turn gazed back at Green as she took hold of her hands and shook her head, "Not at the expense of you and our other sisters, not to mention the vast communities of our world.

28

I am the big sister and it is my job to protect you all, not the other way around."

And so the eldest Oracle became aglow with lunar light before vanishing from her sister's arms.

Chapter 6
Creating the Warriors of Piathos

Meanwhile, back at the Oracles Temple, White paced back and forth anxiously as she gazed on and off from the Great Sigh.

"What must I do, O' Celestial Artefact?" she asked while nervously strutting around inside of the tower.

Suddenly, outside of the Blue Caves at the sea bay, Black remerged upon the force of the moonlight power. Dropping her hood, she turned her gaze to the temple and listened to the constant humming of the crystal ball as White begged and pleaded for its help.

"White," Black whispered before stepping back into the temple where she once again ascended upwards through the stone-coiled stairwell to where her sister pondered anxiously.

Turning away from the crystal ball as her sister stepped foot into the tower, White glanced at Black and let out a long sigh of relief, "Sister, I implore you! Tell me where you have been!"

Taking a moment to gather her thoughts, Black draws in a deep breath before commencing to explain.

"I needed answers, dear sister. And now that I have them, I am more confused than ever. Why did father want to keep this from me?" she asked, on the verge of panic.

White then reluctantly shook her head as she moved away from the crystals' side and elegantly glided towards her sister, Black. Her long, silky-white frock flowed behind her like the wings on a swan as she spoke, "Sister, it is not so simple. If you help in defeating The Nothing, then you could risk becoming more twisted than even he is."

White clasped her hands together with Black's and let out a trembling sigh which was full of guilt.

"Father only desires that we do not see too much. But when I foresaw this coming, I knew that it was up to him to decide the fate of his most precious creations."

"What about our destiny to protect and nurture everything that comes under our power?" Black asked as she pulled back from her sister and turned her gaze to that of the Great Sight.

Smiling over at her sister with the uttermost admiration, White sighed in response.

"Fate and destiny are but two very different things. Although they have similar boundaries, no one can prevent the sun from rising through the black of night, nor can they stop the moon from emerging through the white lights of day. So I express, that father only wanted to protect that which he loves and cherishes most of all."

Black pondered her sister's statement for a moment as she turned her gaze away from the Celestial Artefact and back to meet the gaze of White.

"Then there is but one last task we must enact without our father's blessing."

Nodding at her sister in response, White turned to the Book of Ancients and opened its grand, golden binding and revealed its glowing hallowed pages.

***

Meanwhile, deep within the depths of the ocean, Blue began to council by the Coral Kingdom with her tribespeople and their leader, Titanium.

"Take shelter within the whirlpool boundary that I provide here for your own safety," the Oracle said as she whipped up a whirling barricade so to protect her Tiger Shark tribe.

Titanium also gathered his tribe and rounded them into the protection of the vortex's area.

"This is our home. The home of the Tiger Shark people! Do not flee! Do not be scared for we are a noble tribe!" he extolled his fellow warriors, his voice echoing through the rippling currents.

"My people, rest assure that my sisters and I are working together to restore the order of our kin which we are compelled to protect. Your chief will do everything in his power to maintain your great nation!" Blue declared as the merpeople swam to the safety of her whirlpool barricade.

"It may not be long before all of this turns to nothing." Titanium says as he unsheathes his glistening silver sword.

"I'm afraid that you may be right, Titanium. But I have extended an invitation to the leader of the Great White tribe so that we may speak this out in peace," Blue responded as the changing water currents flowed through her ginger and turquoise hair.

"Be ready for I sense something moving towards us on the tides."

Searching and studying the currents up ahead, Titanium suddenly spotted the most obscure and sinister of motion.

"Eel...!" He warned. "Man the boundaries!"

The huge, black-scaled and yellow-eyed Eel quickly swam and swarmed through the murky waters followed closely by the Great White clan.

"Charge...!" Titanium roared as he rushed out from the safety of Blue's barricade.

"So much for a peaceful conversation," Blue muttered to herself as she magically fortified the area which was protecting the young and elderly tribe's folk.

'O' aqua, Impenitri Isolvox, aguring.'

The sound of wailing and war cries could suddenly be heard for miles under the sea, echoing through the eruption of battle as the waters were violently disturbed with the collision of melee and weaponry combat.

Blue gazed out, looking closely at the giant Eel as they swarmed. Their faces were distorted, showing a malicious and disturbing grin. Their yellow, glowing eyes were menacing and truly demonic. Their satanic faces posed no fear for the Tiger Shark tribe as Titanium charged through the opposing merfolk and their sea beasts with his large, sharp horns...

***

Back in the forest, Green had gone to council with her woodland folk, when she had noticed that the air around her elven village had become tainted with a rather potent and oddly unpleasant smell.

"My kin, please do not hide!" Green called out as she stood front and centre of the woodland village, "For I need your help if we are to protect ourselves."

"We know not of battle, my lady," Woodflower commented as she stepped into the clearing of moonlight to stand with her goddess.

"We are a peaceful and humble nation just as you are beautiful and soft, Your Excellency."

"Nonsense," Green says. "If you believe in this peace that we all want, then we must fight for it. We may not be a daring people like the merfolk but we are no strangers to strength either."

Woodflower turned to the elves that were scattered all around their forest village before returning her gaze towards Green and asking, "What should we do?"

"Gather as many willing soldiers as you can," Green began, "take to the mountains where you will find the fair folk and the Dragons. Call to your elven brethren, both the Lunar and the Solar Mystic alike."

"And what of you my lady...?" Woodflower implored.

"I'll stay here and protect those that cannot fend for themselves," the Oracle smiled as she gently placed her hand atop the wood elf's face.

Suddenly, the potent smell of death and decay grew all the more formidable as from the shadows of the woodland came stomping an army of giants and trolls.

Green turned her gaze to the intruders as the winds around her suddenly took up, carrying the youngest Oracle into the air where she used the gusts to guide her in flight.

'O' sapphire, lio morbos, don, impenitri isolvox, gio. '

The young Oracle chanted as she summoned electrical vines that sprouted up from the ground to stun and immobilise her enemies, giving her elves a quick and easy chance of escaping the assault.

***

Meanwhile back at the Temple of the Oracles, both Black and White stood together with their hands joined over the Book of Ancients as they called upon the Celestial Forces.

'O' great Artefact, we call upon your gift, aid us through the dark and balance out the light.'

The sisters spoke in unison and as they continued to chant together, the Great Sight suddenly began to come aglow and as it glistened, its crystal exterior melted away to reveal a bubble of liquid light with images of a world that only humans could know as home.

"What is that?" Black gasped, bewildered and mystified as she and White steadily approached the gleaming Artefact.

"Look there!" White sighed as she gazed out, wide-eyed at the most beautiful blue world that was orbiting a golden star in the distant image of outer space.

"It is the young planet, dear sister. The one that all beings from different worlds inhabit together in peace…"

Black smiled with relief as she and White both gazed out at the foreign world's image through the Great Sight's surface in awe.

"It is the planet Earth, dear sister," Black breathed.

"Then it is time," White said as she returned to the Book of Ancients.

Taking to the treasury within their tower, Black pulled from the sacred cupboards a handful of Divine Artefacts both of Celestial and Mystical properties.

And from their trove, Black collected a set of silver gauntlets, a clear-jewelled tiara, an emerald headpiece, a white-feathered necklace that had silver chaining and a silver bracelet that was laced with clear Piolan gemstones.

She also gathered together a magical belt which was coated in black leather and had dark fur that gathered near the red-ruby button, a stunning pair of silver, dual ear jewels that twisted and coiled like snakes, a golden, red-feathered quiver, a glacier-steel sword and a glowing-blue trident.

"This is everything that we will need for the spell, dear sister," Black muttered as she floated the Divine Artefacts around the Great Sight.

White smiled to herself as she pulled the book from its stand and brought the golden glowing Artefact over to where her sister stood.

"This is the spell, dear sister; a spell that will allow us to augment a small army of brave and loyal hearts."

Black grinned back at her sister as she waved her hand at the Artefacts which were hovering around the Great Sight in an orbit like planets to a star.

"Are you ready for this?" the eldest Oracle asked.

'For the Earth, may you bare the Warriors that destiny needs and may you gift them with these Artefacts. Bind them to their powers upon age through time and space.
Fire, tether with the quiver to find balance when calm collides with chaos,
Water to the trident, so the soft can meet the current.'

The sisters chanted rhythmically with each other while adding the Artefacts to the Great Sight which had become a bubble of liquid light.

'Lightning to this bracelet, may you conduct the will to control.
Plant life with the emerald, may the turmoil rest to tranquil.
Cryo to the sword, may the frost submerge with heat.
Serenity to this crown, may mind become the focus.
Mist to the snakes, may the cunning become the complete.'

They continued as one by one the sisters dropped the Artefacts into the bubble which was showing the passage of outer space.

'Great power and strength seal the belt.
Winds, bind the chains of this necklace piece, submerge the
sublime to flow with serene.
Energy, infuse these mighty gauntlets, and bring balance to
these beings blessed.'

And just as the sisters added the last ingredient, the Great Sight suddenly became aglow with brighter light before sealing over and becoming solid crystal once again.

"By the heavens, it worked..." Black smiled softly while giving a long sigh of relief. "No matter what happens now, dear sister, my future here can be saved regardless of the outcome..."

Chapter 7
The Fires of Judgement

As Piathos bled into the darkness of night, Andreas stood still, watching over the world beyond his city borders. Filling with anguish and dismay, he gazed on from a balcony high within in his castle chambers, waiting for his daughters to return to him with the Book of Ancients.

Suddenly, the sound of clapping resonated from behind the King as he waited patiently within his castle chambers.

"Truly remarkable isn't it…" Eclipse spoke from Andreas' doorway, "this had to be done your highness. As time, it is not meant to be at a standstill. Not for the eternal force of a living entity."

King Andreas turned to meet Eclipse's steely-eyed gaze as the pale-skinned Lunar Mystic sharply glared back at him.

"What manner of creatures have you unleashed upon the unsuspecting people of these lands?" the King asked.

"Whatever do you mean?" Eclipse asked coyly, "If I remember correctly, the giants and trolls are people of these lands too, your grace…"

"Why are you saying things like this, Eclipse? I thought you were my ally! I thought you were my friend…!" the King spoke while unsheathing his amazing Arcane Sword.

"I was never really your ally, Andreas; I was never really your friend. But then again, after all these years of my charm, you always knew better," the Lunar Mystic chuckled as he pulled from his belt, a dark, long sword of pulsing ominous energy.

"I had this Dark Artefact forged for me by the crones of the ancient far lands," Eclipse gloated.

"The crones of the ancient far lands," Andreas chuckled as he and Eclipse began to circle each other. "I thought that they were all dead?"

"For an Archangel, you are not the most perceptive of beings, Andreas Feather," Eclipse scoffed, "after all, it was those old sorcerers that helped in providing a birthing cauldron for you to create the Oracle sisters."

"You know as well as I that the crones of the ancient far lands only care about supremacy and being in favour of those that hold great power," Andreas responded as he steadily made pace towards the Lunar Mystic. "After the Oracles were born however, the crones slowly started to die out. It is rather funny considering that it was me that was putting them out when they insisted on aiding The Nothing to purge me of this land."

"And for that reason, they have favoured to champion me..." Eclipse chuckled as he twirled his new, dark blade around in his hand, "And so, I am reborn, one of The Nothing's messengers. His first Dark Priest!"

"I'll give him your regards when I lock him away for another thousand years," Andreas sharply responded as he and Eclipse quickly flew into battle.

Sparking with holy lightning and fire, King Andreas' chamber quickly became aglow with Celestial light so bright and intense that the force it radiated was enough to throw Eclipse free of the castle and into the citadel below.

Blooming into his greater form, Andreas swooped high above the City of Angels dressed in the most intense of ethereal armour, which seemed to reflect that of the stars of daylight in the cosmos, even though there was no day sky in sight. He spread open two pairs of majestic dark-feathered wings and then he spread open another and another until his entire body was being carried by six sublime wings that resembled that of an immense cloak and trail cape.

Standing from his fall and covered in holy burns, Eclipse began to crack his bones back into place before gazing up at the almighty Celestial who was gliding down to meet him in the citadel below.

"My deal with Zealous is absolute!" Eclipse screamed in anger as Andreas illuminated brightly like a beacon of hope in the darkness of night.

"What do you think, King Andreas? I cannot be killed so easily..." he mocked.

Gazing upon the true satanic beast Eclipse had finally become, Andreas closed away his wings as he walked towards the maniacal and burned moon elf.

"You really sold your soul, didn't you?"

"It comes with certain perks," Eclipse cackled while retrieving his dark sword from the ground, "I can fly..."

Taking to the skies in an aura of glowing purple energy, the dark-fuelled Lunar Mystic goaded the King into reopening his wings so as to join him on the breeze for an airborne battle of sword duelling.

***

Meanwhile on the ground, Black had arrived at the City of Angels with the Book of Ancients in hand as she materialised into the citadel using her powers of lunar transportation. She knew that they didn't have long before The Nothing's re-emergence and that her own people were left to the mercy of Eclipse and his traitorous actions. All the while, White was left to gather the Lunar Mystics as well as the Solar Mystics and the fey that dwelt within the Veil of the Fairies between the two great mountains.

Sparing no time, Black began to make way for her father's castle as the King and the traitor crossed their mighty blades chaotically above the city grounds.

Spotting the Oracle as she made her way for the castle through the city grounds, Eclipse grinned menacingly while swooping out of the King's range and taking aim at her with the dark magics of his evil sword.

"Black, get out of there!" Andreas cried out, alerting his daughter to the immediate danger.

'O' shadow, impenitri Isolvox.'

She called out while holding up her left hand. Suddenly and to King Andreas' relief, Black was quickly shielded by a darkly glistening aura of lunar and shadowy energy.

"Bring me the book!" Andreas exclaimed as he swooped down to grab the Celestial Artefact from her hands.

Hissing and snarling, Eclipse then plummeted down in a frantic dive of panic as Black successfully handed the Book of Ancients to her father.

"Time to rid this world of you, Eclipse, there is no goodnight in this light." Andreas spoke with a coy expression as he opened the golden binding of the book to reveal its glowing and radiant interior.

"You cannot do this Andreas, I am immortal!" the manic Lunar Mystic exclaimed before taking another dive at the King, with his sword pointed forward.

'O' Celestial forces to you I pray, bring forward your light! Cast what's evil away.'

The King read proudly from the pages within the Book of Ancients.

Then suddenly, an immense explosion erupted from within the pages of the book. With a tremendous force, Black was knocked over and flung several feet from where she was standing.

Eclipse was struck down from where he flew. The blinding and pure Celestial light shone so intensely and full of might that it completely obliterated the dark-fuelled moon elf into a pile of ash. And once the glowing blaze had settled from the blast, the charred cindered remains of Eclipse were then quickly blown away by the whooshing aftermath of the spell, thanks to the wonderful magics that came from within the pages of Book of Ancients.

Chapter 8
A Painful Sunrise

And so, as dawn approached over what should have been a beautiful morning at the Oracles Temple, the surviving factions of the sisters' people all gathered together near the ocean caves at the sea bay.

"How could all of this have happened in just one night?" Green sighed while gazing out at the hordes of Dragons, fairies, merfolk and elves that were together, gathering around their sacred home.

"It was all planned, set up right under our noses," King Andreas' great voice resonated as he ascended from the skies with Black in his arms.

"It appears that the Lunar Mystic, Eclipse, was behind everything."

And, as the great King landed with a whoosh on the soil of the ground, Black commenced to step forward and address the seriousness of what Eclipse had brought to the Lunar people's gracious name.

"I implore to any and all of my people to speak out if they had somewhat of an idea to what Eclipse had been planning?" Black spoke clearly as the indistinct voices of the people continue to echo from near and far across the bay.

"Treachery amongst my kin is prohibited and will be punishable by being stripped of their magics and banished to the far lands."

Titanium and his beautiful mermaid wife, named Hope, swam through the waters of their wailing people and approached the four Oracle sisters who stood together on land. The distinct difference in appearance between the genders of merpeople, is that mermen harbour powerful and sharp vertical fishtails that allow for land traversal and climbing, as well as the two pointed horns that grow from their heads like antlers when they reach the age of maturity; mermaids, on the other hand, are traditionally softer in appearance and have very elegant horizontal fins, which help them to move more fluidly while hunting or fighting under the sea.

"Today Piathos bleeds, everywhere I look I see all but woe and strife in the hearts of the people from all different nations here," the angered merman declared. "In this time of grief, my forces of the ocean would gladly join you in the fight to right this wrong."

The sisters gazed upon the brave aquatic warrior who had pulled himself up onto the beach to stand tall beside them. Using the might of his fishtail, Titanium pulled himself upwards in a strong stance so as to meet the Oracle sisters eye to eye.

Blue smiled proudly upon him as she commenced forward to meet his gaze, "Titanium, you truly are a man amongst many."

King Andreas, too, smiled with admiration at the chief of the Tiger Shark tribe as he opened out his extraordinary heavenly wings and drew in a deep breath.

"People of Piathos, hear me now. From the City of Angels, to the vast forests of Green and the mountains of Mystics both Lunar and Solar alike, as well as the tribes of oceans deep!" Andreas began. "In this time of dismay, I will most humbly ask, are you willing to join me and stand against the dark forces of The Nothing as did your ancestors, many moons ago?"

"My tribe's folk and I are yours to command, O' Great King! Lead us forth and help us right this wrong!" Titanium responded while slithering across the sand at the bay, his horns still stained with the blood of his enemies from the night before.

Just then, a very handsome, young wood elf with long, brown, braided hair and striking green eyes stepped forward from amongst his people and proudly approached the King with an expression of contentment on his face.

"I too wish to join your ranks, King Andreas. Your enemy is my enemy, and I want to defend the peers of my home as well as the people of the nation's afar!" the wood elf exclaimed.

"What is your name, wood elf?" Green asked while gazing upon his handsome face.

The wood elf turned his attention to the youngest Oracle and bowed his head before the goddess.

"My name is Wisdom, my lady. And I humbly lay my life before your greatness."

Green turned a distinct shade of red as she smiled upon the dashing wood elf to who was gazing back at her with a kind but intense gaze.

As the day passed on, the tribespeople of the sea soon began to work side by side with any and all wood elves that were willing to go forth into combat. Training them in hand-held weaponry, the mermen and mermaids quickly began to teach the basics of sword warfare as well as archery and basic bow-staff fighting to the far less-experienced elven kind.

"Wisdom, come forth and accept my gift," Green proudly projected while holding out her left hand to greet him.

"Green, I am yours in any way that you desire, my lady," the blushing wood elf sighed while kneeling down before Green within her chambers at the Oracles Temple.

"Stand brave elf," she said. "I seek out a new keeper of the Dragons. And I, Green, Oracle of the land and sky, implore you to be their great and loyal new master."

Wisdom's heart then became filled with astonishment as he glanced upward towards Green, wide-eyed with awe.

A quiet moment passed before Green stepped forward and planted a gentle kiss atop his soft and pale skin. "A token of my gratitude, for your fealty, Wisdom…"

Wisdom nodded his head before taking the Oracle's right hand and returning the gentle kiss. "And a token of my admiration, milady, so may you fare well in this noble fight."

Chapter 9
This Is War

And as the world of Piathos drifted off into the shadow of another long night, the almighty and wonderful King Andreas gathered round the council of his four precious daughters, deep within the confines of his castle.

"Blue, you must carry the Tiger Shark tribe away from the coral below the Blue Caves and take them further into the vast wilds of the ocean," the King spoke, "that way they will have the element of surprise when the Great Whites and their beasts return."

"Yes, father," Blue says with a smile before evaporating into water and flying off towards the sea bay where Titanium and his tribe awaited for her solemn return.

The King swivelled his silver-blue eyes to Green and said, "My darling child, I need you to fortify my city with a forest like no other. Take to the lands below and the skies above, use the might of all elven kind that come under you and your two eldest sisters."

"What of the fairies?" Green asked.

"I have protected them with a spell," White responded while holding out a sparkling clear diamond. "And I have bound their home to this Divine Artefact. Their Kingdom will not be breached."

Green then passed a soft smile for luck towards her older sister before whirling off into a vortex of wind and forest debris.

King Andreas then turned to his second eldest while holding out both of his hands, "Come with me, my darling. For I will need you by my side as I prepare my energies to re-imprison the foul darkness of The Nothing."

White nodded her head at her father before glancing back at Black with an expression of ambiguity, "And what of Black, father?"

Andreas paused for a moment before turning his attention to his firstborn, "Go home Black. Go back to your temple and stay hidden until all of this has passed."

"But father, my powers can help, I can handle this." Black tried to reason.

"Not at the expense of what could happen to you, my darling..." Andreas said while pressing his hands atop her shoulders.

"But father!" she exclaimed sharply.

"Just stay hidden and protect the Great Sight," Andreas finished before using his magic to whisk her back into her chambers that lay within the Oracles Temple.

Soon realising that she was sent back home, Black let out a rather sharp and high-pitched scream which shattered the glass of her giant stone windows.

"Show me again," she grunted while storming back out of her chambers and ascending the stone-coiled steps that lead up towards the tower that sat atop their temple.

***

Meanwhile, in the vast waves of the choppy Piolan seas, Blue, Titanium and the rest of the Tiger Shark warriors waited by the moonlit surface for the arrival of the Sea-Dragons and Titanium's brothering tribe.

***

And elsewhere by the Mystic Mountains, Green stood idle under an old willow tree waiting for the enemy to return, all the while accompanied by Woodflower and Wisdom who were, in actual fact, adopted mother and son.

"Our forces are ready, my lady," Wisdom decreed. "Once all of the other elves have manned their stations, then I will take to the skies on the back of my new friend."

Both Woodflower and Green then gazed up to the skies as the most majestic, glistening, red-scaled Dragon swooped down towards them, picking up strong gusts of wind and forest debris as it landed.

"Ladies," he spoke, "I'd like you to meet, the big, red Dragon!"

Woodflower chuckled while Green blushed as she twirled her fingers through her hair.

"I long to see your heroism, young Wisdom, please be safe," the young Oracle muttered.

"For you, my lady, I will fight a hundred trolls and giants a thousand times over!" he fluttered in response while passing a cocky wink back at her.

***

Back in the sea, Blue spoke to the tribe with a short and sharp speech so as to motivate the soldiers before commencing forth into battle.

"Rest assure, for you are the finest warriors of the Tiger Shark tribe! On this day, we fight for the freedom of not only the sea but for the world of Piathos itself!"

'O' aqua, hydro le pen Impenitri isolvox.'

The Oracle chanted, and from the choppy seas came mighty gallons of swirling aquatic vortexes that shot high up into the night sky. Hazing out the clear, starry view in a flurry of soft and steamy hot mist, the hydro barricades continued to rise.

"This should protect the young and the elderly so that they wouldn't have to worry their glistening little fishtails about any danger or any harm ever coming too close to them. No one is getting in or out of my sanctuary spell," Blue said.

From the distance of the ocean's currents echoed the serene sounding songs of the Sea-Dragons as they hopped and jumped through the waves like a family of dolphins. Their tropical, glittering scales twinkled and sparkled under the shining of the Piolan moonlight as they approached the Tiger Shark tribe with an army of allies and friends.

"My brother Seafire and the great warriors of the Hammer Head tribe! You grace us with your presence at last!" Titanium laughed as he and his brother happily embraced each other with a hug.

Seafire was also a very sturdy and powerful merman that graced the waves with ferocity and mighty strength. And to show off his strength, around his neck, he wore a chain that harboured the daringly sharp teeth of every monster Eel that he had ever slain.

"It is good to see you again too, Titanium," the muscular, dark-skinned redhead spoke.

"Indeed Seafire, it has been almost an entire lifetime since we last drew our swords together, side by side in battle!" the leader of the Tiger Sharks laughed.

"Indeed, it has," Seafire responded in kind.

***

All the while back at the twin Mountains of the Mystics, Green had taken into flight once again, high above the City of Angels she glided while using her magic to surround and fortify her father's home with a deadly growth of greenery and forest fortitude.

'O' Sapphire, impenitri isolvox, lio morbos gio estungi eirtiti, impenitri isolvox don forth plantus celuni.'

And so, Green's spell grew far and wide around the city as a circle of forest spiralled round and round, protecting the Kingdom from the intrusion of any and all harmful invaders.

Glancing out of the windows from the depths of the sealed tomb entrance where The Nothing lingered deep within the darkness like a caged animal, White quickly turned to her father as the might of Green's formidable forest continued to stretch in a sphere around the great and holy metropolis.

"Green is casting her spell, father. The castle has now been fortified," White said as she continued to watch over Andreas.

"Good. Then it is time to begin my transcendence," the King muttered as he pricked his finger on the point of his Arcane Sword so that he could draw the Celestial blood required for the Book of Ancients spell in summoning the power needed to re-imprison The Nothing.

"You have the power of the light, my daughter," Andreas spoke, "you can fend off his coming while I commence forth with this extremely sensitive and complex ritual."

"Be well, father," White nodded as she gazed on at Andreas with fear and dread in her eyes.

***

In the Oracles Temple, Black stood still, tarrying as she gazed longingly into the gleaming crystal surface of the Great Sight as it sat upon its perch and sparkled in the moonlight that shone through from the windows that stood above the altar.

Suddenly from its core, came a very strange and unusual pulsing of warm Celestial light. Black gazed on, deeply into the gleaming waves as it enticed her to surrender before it and become enthralled by its wholesome and compelling calling…

'Let there be light.'

A strange male voice sounded in an echo of waves as Black found herself floating through what appeared to be a new-born galaxy of swirling baby stars.

"Where am I?" the eldest Oracle asked while floating down to what appeared to be the sea bay of her home at the Blue Caves just outside of the Oracles Temple.

Glancing around at her surroundings however, Black noticed that everything was glowing with luminescent light and was foggy in gaze to focus on.

"Is this real?" she whispered.

'What you see before you is what you perceive as safe for now.'

The voice spoke calmingly to her.

"Hello?" Black asked. Her voice was resonating with that of the entity which was talking to her in kind.

'Black, listen to me Black.'

The soothing voice continued to resonate with the luminescent glow of the world in a sensory calm.

'The Nothing lingers alone in the shadows unable to see. But his prison in time is just not meant to be. Though once he is free before the breaking of dawn, he will siphon upon all that the light of day shines upon.'

The voice continued.

And as Black gazed around at the dreamlike dazzle of her once and sacred home, she soon realised that the words that were spoken to her were in fact the words of Eternia himself.

"I don't understand." Black said as she continued to search around with her eyes.

'Look inside of yourself, Black. The answer is already there. When exposed to the light, he shall rain down despair. But if sheltered in shadow, The Nothing shall see nothing at all, but rendered in sleep.'

The words spoken to the Oracle echoed through her mind as the sensory glow of the world around her melted away and transformed back into the vast, swirling galaxy of baby stars.

Suddenly, becoming alert and awakening within the tower of her temple, Black quickly realised that in order to save everyone on the entire planet, she would in fact have to surrender herself to the fate of her own hero's journey.

"What is this?" she pondered while gazing down at her hand to see a small crystallised shard gleaming in the glow of the Piolan full moon.

Black then turned her gaze towards the stand to where the Great Sight was stationed and realised that the Celestial Artefact was no longer there. She then turned to the crystal piece that was sitting in her hand and pondered deeply to herself while studying its surface to see its dazzling gleam gazing back at her.

"Incredible," she sighed before heading to the treasure trove that was allocated within the temple's tower. And from their sacred cupboards, Black retrieved a silver linked chain which she then magically bonded the crystal to, therefore creating an entirely new Artefact, the Celestial Crystal Necklace.

***

During this time, beyond the mysterious isle and between the Twin Mountains, the youngest Oracle Green waited in the shadows for the enemy to return from the far lands. She pondered silently with her collective army of magically infused Mystics as well dozens of wood elves and fierce, fire-breathing Dragons.

"My lady," Wisdom exclaimed as he came whooshing down from the skies on the back of his red-scaled Dragon, "the enemy fast approaches and they are headed right for the City of Angels."

"Then we attack," Green responded, taking flight once again, "Wisdom and I will man the skies, while everyone else shall take refuge in the forest that blooms around the city. Come at them from the shelter that I have provided. No mercy to those who are in service to The Nothing."

As Wisdom soared on the breeze side by side with Green, the pair suddenly came under attack by a hoard of aladon demons. Their sharp webbed wings were cutting through the air as they swarmed the night sky like a group of giant humanoid bats.

"Alright Big Red, let's get them!" Wisdom yelled as he and his dragon swooped around the wailing flock at high speeds. The Dragon complied with its new master and friend as it began drawing in a deep breath of air before quickly expelling from its snout a giant vortex of searing, hot flames upon the flittering group of screeching creatures.

'O' sapphire, electro.'

Green chanted while ripping a few hundred volts of intense thunder and lightning from the night sky, through an extraordinary display of a magically infused storming tempest.

Shrieking from the fiery and electrical assaults, the aladon demons quickly began to scatter, allowing for Wisdom to draw his brand new sword of Tiger Shark craftsmanship.

***

Elsewhere, under the depths of the Piolan Sea, the Tiger Shark and Hammer Head tribes waited eagerly for battle on the backs of their beautiful yet powerful aquatic Dragons.

"Change is on the tides," Blue spoke as she glided around her circular prism which protected the young and elderly from any and all harm. "They are here..."

From the shadows of the underwater current came the eerie grinning faces of the demonic Eels, as they slithered through the weaving tides, accompanied by the silver-scaled warriors of the Great White tribe.

Suddenly, swimming in unison with each other, both Titanium and Seafire charged forth ramming their horns through the bodies of many opposing enemies, all while the Dragons spewed boiling hot water and freezing cold pulses from their mouth upon the unkindly and demonic Eels.

Quickly locking horns in an underwater tug, the mermen on each side began to tackle and tear into each other as the sea currents quickly became foggy with a red haze of gushing blood. Many mermaids too began to swim out into battle, the ocean floor coming alive with the echoes and chaos of swordplay and underwater warfare.

The battle was fierce, and the warriors were brave, though the casualties were quickly growing as countless bodies of friend and foe alike soon fell limp and drifted off into the shadows and down to their watery graves on the ocean floor below.

***

The struggles above the sea shores and vast lands wide, bled chaotically into the darkness of night, as though the land were lamenting its predicament.

Although usually a gentle-natured people, the wood elves of Green's valley fought valiantly and with great honour against the giants and trolls that attempted to breach the mighty walls of the City of Angels.

Many Lunar and Solar Mystics used their magics to fend off the beasts' heads on while the wood elves moved stealthily with the Dragons amongst the vines and limbs of Green's fortified forest.

Meanwhile, as the sounds of swordplay and war cries could be heard echoing vastly around the city walls, Green and Wisdom remained high on the breeze of flight, combining their forces to keep the demons away from their King's mighty castle as he meditated.

"I could get used to this glory!" Wisdom laughed while swooping round and around on the waves of night air gusts. Though his skills were admirable and his aim was true, Wisdom soon found himself on the sharp end of an aladon demon's claw. The spike of its wing punctured the centre of his young body, right through his chest.

"No!" Green exclaimed as a giant flock of the demons quickly surrounded her in a flurry of sharp, flapping webbed wings. Wisdom gazed helplessly at her as he quickly bled out. His eyes grew tired as he fell limp from the Dragon's back and plummeted silently through the hazy wisps of the clouds high above in the night sky.

Quickly becoming enraged by what she had just witnessed, Green called upon a spell of thundering tempests so that she could clear a path of the shrieking beasts and catch Wisdom as he fell.

'O' sapphire, electro.'

From the heavens above them, the aladon demons quickly found themselves being struck by the extreme forces of thunder and lightning. And as the web-winged creatures fell burning out of the night sky, Green began to plummet downward towards the ground to where she found the red-scaled Dragon holding onto the wood elf as he bled.

Gazing up in anger at the demon that had just impaled Wisdom, Green held out her hands and summoned the power to destroy the unholy monstrosity as it flapped its way towards the castle.

'O' sapphire, incenderie.'

The fleeting demon that circled the air high above the city grounds quickly burst into flames as it soared, and so Green watched on with eyes of anguish and rage as it screamed out in pain before falling in circles to the ground where it exploded on impact, just beyond the castle walls.

"Did we get them?" Wisdom murmured while shivering in shock. His blood poured freely from his chest and mouth as he struggled to speak.

"Ssh, save your strength, Wisdom," Green whispered as she laid him down on the ground in the woodlands of his people's home. The red-scaled Dragon too curled up beside him as it trilled and whimpered softly in sorrow.

"I am so happy that I finally got to fly side by side with the goddess of our nation," Wisdom said with a smile before his prone form turned cold and fell still.

"Wisdom..." Green sobbed as the indistinct sounds of battle continued to rage on in the distance of the forest wilds, near and far.

Unknown to the youngest Oracle however, that as she continued to cry out in woe, Wisdom's body unexpectedly began to repair itself as Green's tears of grief suddenly commenced in reviving the recently fallen soldier of his mortal and fatal wounds.

Suddenly from his eternal slumber, with a gasp, Wisdom lunged forward from lying still in the young Oracle's arms. Green gasped with astonishment as the young wood elf redrew, what was supposed to be, his final living breath.

"By the heavens..." Green signed as she and the Dragon gazed on in bewilderment at the revival of the young and brave wood elf.

Chapter 10
The Sleeping Cast

Back at the castle however, White pondered on as Andreas continued to muster the Celestial magics required to reshape his prism of time. The King slowly began to fall under the thrall of his ever-growing, white glowing aura of whooshing and angelic powers, as the time loop that sealed Zealous in his prison slowly began to weaken and break away.

Watching on as her father fell into his slumbering trance of serenity, White paced back and forth anxiously within the cold and dingy, stone dungeon deep within the castle confines, all the while the sounds of battle continued to resonate from the world outside.

Suddenly from the ground beneath them, oozed up a black-bloodied substance which was so hot that it began to mist and smoke as it rose in a stench so foul that it would sicken even the dead...

White froze up in terror where she stood, as the stone crust only a few feet away from her suddenly began to crumble and melt away.

As the Oracle looked up, the grey-skinned entity began to pull himself free of the dark void that was holding him prisoner for many thousands of years. His long, sharp, claw-like nails gave a bloodcurdling screech as he climbed up out of the darkness to join White in the light where she stood.

"At long last, I am free..." The Nothing sighed as he opened his black, empty eyes and drew in a deep breath of fresh night air. His body was skinny to the bone as he stood before the Oracle dressed in the most frayed of black, torn cloth.

"Zealous...?" White muttered while trembling in the presence of his eternal hollowness.

"Well, well…" He said while breathing through a raspy and cold corpse-like grin, "a witch. You, my precious, are only but a copy of the one true Oracle that will rise and meet me on the horizon in the cosmos afar."

White shook her head in an attempt to break free of the shock paralysis before turning her gaze onward to the King as he continued to slumber in trance.

"Father…!" she called out to him like a lost child that was frightened and alone in the darkness.

"Your father," The Nothing said as he turned to see that King Andreas still consumed the light and its forces from the gleaming pages of the Book of Ancients that lay open before him, radiating a powerful aura. "It appears that the great and mighty Archangel, Andreas Feather, was not so quick to stop me this time," Zealous chuckled as he reached out his bony, branch-like hands so as to touch and siphon the King as he slumbered.

White lunged before her father and in a desperate attempt to halt The Nothing, she immediately began to cast her offensive and defensive spells.

'O' light, le pen don soler.'

In an extreme flash of sunlight, the entity was instantly struck and vaporised by the utmost intense of heat and solar ray light.

White quickly turned to her father, who was almost completely finished drawing the power from the Book of Ancients and whispered softly into his ear while plucking a sparking diamond bracelet from her right hand, "please hurry."

She then placed the bracelet down beside the King and began to cast a spell of protection as The Nothing slowly began to reform, bigger and stronger, from the mist and dark blood that he had originally risen from.

'O' light, impenitri isolvox, celuni soler.'

White chanted while using her bracelet to anchor her father into a sphere of radiant and glistening energy.

Finally remerging larger and stronger from soaking up the energy by which he was struck, the now more human-appearing Zealous grinned coyly at her and said, while holding out his soft and pink, pale hand, "Are you afraid of me, my darling?"

His eyes were now blue and oddly enchanting to gaze upon.

'O' light, le pen don soler.'

Struck again with the intense heat and light, The Nothing was quickly evaporated into a cloud of mist only meters away from where White stood.

"Father, please hurry," the Oracle trembled as she implored him, "I cannot hold him forever."

Appearing from the second blast, Zealous remerged more enchantingly soft, focused and beautiful than ever before. He cast his gaze upon White with soft and enthralling blue eyes, he spoke, "You know, White, is it?" he smiled softly, "You remind me of my darling wife. Her name is Red and she is the Celestial Oracle of the cosmos. I only wish to retrieve her and bring her to your world so that we may live our lives together in peace…"

White wavered like a flickering candle as she stood between her father and The Nothing who continued to attempt to seduce and distract her.

"I only have to hold off your coming…" she said with trembling anger.

'O' light, le pen don soler.'

And from the third blast Zealous was remade into a sublime and stunning image of sheer godly perfection.

"You know that you can no longer resist me," The Nothing smirked playfully.

"Daddy…" White winced as the smooth-robed and devilishly handsome young man slowly made pace towards her.

"Do not fret, my darling," The Nothing whispered intimately as he stood mere inches from her face, "for it is time to bring everyone around to my way of thinking…"

Suddenly and ominously, The Nothing began to release a fluffy pale mist from his entire body which danced around White like an alluring flurry of pleasant dreams.

"No one will be able to resist me…" he said in a seductive tone.

White turned away from The Nothing as she felt herself becoming consumed by his pleasant charms. In one last effort to evade him, she lunged behind the sphere barrier with her father and waited for him to complete the magics of his transcendence.

***

Meanwhile, as Green and Wisdom remained hidden deep within the forest fortress, the pair had suddenly noticed that a strange fog had started to roll out from within the City of Angels and befall on the land before them.

"What is this?" the young Oracle exclaimed as the mist blew out onto the battlefields of near and far.

"It is the coming of Zealous," Wisdom muttered as he lay tiredly in the Oracle's arms, "our history books speak of the dreamlike haze that follows his re-emergence."

"So, once it touches you…" Green sighed while turning her head to the folks who fought valiantly on the battlegrounds, "you are compelled to touch it back."

"It would seem that the King was too late…" Wisdom sighed as he turned to meet his Dragon's loving gaze, "I am so sorry."

"It is not over just yet," Green said while standing, "I must go to my father and sister. You stay here with your Dragon and remain out of sight," the Oracle spoke as she plucked a lilac flower from her brown and green forest, wavy hair.

'O' sapphire, plantus impenitri isolvox.'

She chanted while creating a magical sphere of defensive green energy around Wisdom and his Dragon.

"As long as this flower remains intact, then my spell of protection will keep you and your friend safe from all harm," Green muttered while handing the lilac plant to the wood elf that lay weakened on the grass beside his red-scaled Dragon.

"What about you?" Wisdom asked as he gazed up at the young Oracle standing before him.

"Don't worry," she smiled, "I can avoid the haze's touch, for now…"

In a whirling vortex of wind, Green quickly vanished from the forest as the clouds and mist continued to spread across the land like a toxic wisp of deathly frost.

As the mist continued to fester across the land, all that had succumbed to its swirling embrace yielded to the will and desire of the revived living entity, The Nothing.

***

"Retreat from the above world! Take refuge on the reef!" Titanium called out as the ghastly fogging haze began to stretch across the surface of the sea waves.

The underwater battle had all but ended with the Tiger Sharks and Hammer Heads standing victorious amongst their peers. The Great White tribe and their monster Eel however, were all beaten to a complete stop and were forced into exile by Blue who had shown them mercy in turn for their surrender.

"This is where we say farewell, Titanium," Blue spoke as she swam side by side with the people of the aquatic tribes, "my presence is needed elsewhere."

Seafire smiled at the Oracle before taking to the depths of the sea with his tribe and Dragons in tow, leaving Titanium and Blue to bid their farewell by silently taking each other in arms as only true warriors do.

"Be well, my lady," Titanium spoke before recalling his people and taking them back to the safety of the coral at bottom of the Blue Caves.

The oceanic Oracle pondered silently for a moment before turning her glance upwards to where the toxic fog was slowly creeping along above the sea shore.

'O' aqua, lio morbos, aguring windempest.'

Blue chanted, as she changed the density of her aqua prism into that of a swirling water flume which exploded upwards out of the surface. The power of the maelstrom sharply cleared a path of the mist so that she could transport herself safely to the City of Angels without the risk of being infected.

***

In the meantime, as the mist carried on across the vast tides of the oceans waves, Black tarried quietly from within the tower's peak, wondering why the sound resonating from the battles that had earlier raged on from the lands far and wide, had stopped.

The eldest Oracle cast her gaze out of the windows of the tower to see that all which walked within her moonlight had become frozen in a strange white mist, surrendered to the uncanny powers of The Nothing's will.

And so, leaving the confines of her sacred home, Black took to the shores at the sea bay just beyond the Oracles Temple and stood idle as the pale misty fog danced towards her from across the choppy waves.

"No more," Black whispered to herself while clutching tightly onto the crystal shard which sat elegantly around her neck. She then drew in a deep breath and closed her eyes as she pondered upon the outcome of her own damnation and how her loss would save the lives and the very souls of the millions of unsuspecting, innocent people.

'May we not be seen or heard, where darkness makes the only sounds, unworthy eyes gaze to our grace, and on their sights an empty page. Cloaked in shadow, shielded in twilight, rest upon easy tides, sleep this world... Sleep in kind.'

Black began to sing her quiet chant, clutching tightly to the crystal shard as she continued ahead with her sleeping cast. As she continued to project her voice across the sea bay, the Celestial Crystal suddenly began to resonate with her vocal tone before carrying her song far and wide into the atmosphere overhead. All who had heard her soothing lullaby as she continued singing were softly rendered off into a gentle and harmless sleep.

Once all beings were finally at rest, Black gazed longingly out at her once sacred home one last time. And as she smiled upon her beautiful world, the tears of acceptance rolled unashamedly down from her face, the moonlight from above shining peacefully down upon the many nations as they slumbered blissfully in sleep.

"If sacrificing my own being this night will help to restore the order of our world, then it shall be done..." Black sighed while studying the silvery gleam of the Piolan full moon, one last time.

As the still moments of serenity passed on, and the fog of The Nothing lay cold on the horizon ahead, Black began to weep and cry for she did not want to lose herself to the twisted will of Zealous. Taking a deep breath, she let go of her fears and woes, all the while preparing her mind for the noble act of banishing the evil which was slowly poisoning her world.

Closing her eyes and clutching tightly onto the crystal shard for solace and strength, Black exhaled. Opening her eyes, Black released her tight grip on the necklace while embracing and accepting the deeds of her solemn and heroic end...

Chapter 11
Black Poison

'O' light incenderie windempest.'

White cast as she conjured a swirling hurricane of searing hot flames to her aid. The force of her firenado was so extreme that it ripped and tore right through the dungeon as it howled and roared into a spinning inferno which caged The Nothing inside the centre of its bright, burning eye.

"Oh, don't be like that White," The Nothing said from within the searing hot blaze, "you are just going to burn yourself out."

Worn out from fighting, White dropped to her knees beside her father as he in turn slowly began to stir.

"I am so tired," she panted, gasping sharply for air.

Suddenly, from the tunnels of the castle came a giant flood of water as Blue had emerged into the dungeon with Green at her side.

'O' aqua, windempest cryogenith lio morbos.'

Blue cast, attempting to trap The Nothing inside of a bubble which quickly became frozen in a giant sphere of solid ice.

"Go now!" Green called out to White who crouched beside the King, "take father and get him to the Isle of the Sea Nymphs!"

Just then, The Nothing began to break free of Blue's cold sphere, melting away the ice, his eyes suddenly started to glow in a searing hot gleam of red.

"Blue," Zealous spoke as he stood in perfection, the ice fading away in a cloud of steam, "I was hoping for more of a warmer welcome. But then again, your sister did beat you to it."

Blue chuckled as she smiled coyly at him, "Oh, but I mean to be cold."

"Foolish girls, your power just feeds me," he chuckled, "Now I intend on taking this world and offering it to Red as her new home."

Stepping from the mist, the sisters could see that The Nothing's body was completely unharmed by the flames or the frost that was inflicted upon him by the powerful Oracle sisters. As he moved to drain the King of his Celestial magics, his feet were in fact melting and burning away at the stone as he walked, leaving scorched footprints in his wake.

'O' sapphire, lio morbos, plantus, impenitri isolvox.'

Green cast while summoning razor-sharp vines up from the ground which tied The Nothing into a knot of agonising and piercing thorns.

"Step aside daughters," Andreas commanded as he rose from his slumber, "it is now time to return you back to the shadows of the void which you came from," the King said as The Nothing slowly began to burn himself free of the vines that bound him, his skin glowing hotly.

Zealous gave a smile of confidence at the King who was standing tall and mighty before him. Andreas stood coated in the most spectacular glow of a golden-white aura, his Celestial Armour gleaming with light as the shining surface of his plating reflected the radiance from the Book of Ancients.

"Get to the Isle of the Sea Nymphs, my girls," Andreas spoke while drawing his extraordinary Arcane Sword, "I won't be far behind you!"

"As ancient as that place is, Andreas," The Nothing said with a smirk, "do you really think that its waters could contain me this time?"

"What choice do we have Zealous?" Andreas muttered.

"You will not stop, you will not yield, and so your love for that goddess has corrupted the balance that you and Eternia once coveted as order. And that order has now been perverted into a twist of chaos."

"Red is not corrupted, Andreas, you are!" The Nothing barked as he once again began to emanate a cloud of swirling mist from his body.

"You will harm no one else, Zealous!" Andreas roared before piercing the tip of his blade into the gut of The Nothing.

Zealous let out a sharp, bloodcurdling cry as the power inside of the Arcane Sword slowly began to draw out the magics which The Nothing had absorbed.

"Your Celestial Artefact won't stop me this time!" The Nothing said as he shoved the king back and began to pull the blade free from his gut, "So here are your two options Andreas. Stop me, or save your world from perishing in my burning rage of Celestial flame."

With a wave of his hand, all of The Nothing's mist began to catch light in a wave of searing hot death, his reign of hellfire swept across the lands and scorching everything for miles within sight. The forest, the lands far and wide, all went up in flames in a second.

"So, what will it be, your grace?" The Nothing laughed as the Oracle sisters stood behind their father, inside the sphere of White's protection spell.

"Imprisoning me or stopping your world and its entire people from burning into ashes."

"No!" Andreas exclaimed as he realised the predicament that he was in.

"That's right Feather. Celestial flames," The Nothing laughed manically, "only the rains dropped upon it from the waters of a Celestial Being can extinguish the fires of my cosmic rage."

"Rrrgh," Andreas groaned before taking to the skies overhead of the blaze.

"Get to the Isle my daughters, you will be safe there!"

And like a sharp, striking fork of lightning, the King bolted into the atmosphere above the clouds where he soared around the entire planet like an angelic hurricane of Celestial power.

"Get to safety, my sisters," White commanded before withdrawing the spell which shielded the Oracles behind a circle of safety.

"I need to find Black," she continued as she retrieved the Book of Ancients from the ground.

Blue and Green both nodded in agreement before whirling from the dungeon as their vortexes of water and wind.

"Back to the Celestial Realm I go," The Nothing spoke as he stood before White in a burning blaze of glorified hellfire.

"Oh, you are not going anywhere, Zealous," White exclaimed before raising her hand to cast upon him.

'O' light, le pen don soler.'

The Nothing violently exploded into a blaze of raging flames that wiped out the lower wing of Andreas' castle. White quickly managed to teleport herself to safety while the City of Angels continued to burn inside of the inferno which Zealous had ignited.

***

Meanwhile, as the Piolan Oracles parted ways, Andreas continued to storm overhead where his Celestial hurricane quickly began to tempest and discharge.

From the clouds above came the purifying Celestial rains as Andreas exerted the forces which he had bonded himself to.

"Green…!" Wisdom exclaimed as he and his Dragon scoured the skies from over the unharmed and ancient mystical Isle of the Sea Nymphs.

"Wisdom," Green gasped as she and Blue approached the haunted, wooden bridge that connected their world to the island. It stood unscathed between the ginormous peaks of the Twin Mystic Mountains.

"What are you doing here? I thought that I had left you safe under my protection spell?"

"I had to get my mother and many others to safety," he responded while soaring down to the ground just beyond the woodland forest.

"I tried to move as many as I could before the flames took them," he said, looking down in sorrow.

Green smiled admirably upon Wisdom as he stood before her in his weakened state, "You are perfectly honourable and extremely brave," she blushed.

"We do not have time for this," Blue exclaimed exasperatedly.

All the while, Andreas' Celestial storm continued to wash heavily down upon them from the skies above.

"We now must enter upon the island. The Nothing's powers will be nullified there as it is the holy place of peaceful passing," Blue explained.

"Nullified?" Green asked with an expression of bewilderment.

"Yes," Blue responded, "if he uses his powers on the island to inflict harm, then the gateway will not grant him access to leave our world."

Mere minutes later, the trio soon found themselves standing on the other side of the haunted, wooden bridge on the Isle of the Sea Nymphs.

"This island is so dreamy," Wisdom sighed as he gazed around at the small orbs of light which floated around the glowing garden like hypnotic spheres of dancing fairy light.

"We will be safe here until The Nothing arrives to travel upon the cosmic seas and back to the Celestial Realm where his bride patiently awaits for his return," Blue muttered before gazing up to see both Black and White standing by the mystical lake which the six Sea Nymph sisters resided upon.

"We cannot allow The Nothing to pass through the ancient gateway. Do not grant him passage to the Celestial Realm," the eldest Nymph spoke as she and her five other sisters walked atop the water's surface.

"Nyx, I am so very glad to see that even you and your sisters understand the severity of this situation," Blue spoke to the dark blue-skinned blonde who flittered atop the mystical waters of their cosmic lake.

"Mother..." the Nymphs exclaimed excitedly as they flurried around the Oracle like an excited litter of adorable puppies.

At that moment, from the stormy skies above, the great King Andreas gently glided down towards the ground just beyond the mystical island as it stood still in the mysterious haze between the Twin Mountains of the Mystic people.

"I am coming for the gateway, Andreas!" The Nothing's voice resounded through the atmosphere as he fast approached the Isle of the Sea Nymphs.

"You have used up all of your stored energy which means you no longer possess the power required to imprison me once again!" Zealous crowed in triumph.

"Meet me on the island, Zealous…" Andreas warned, "You will not get far…"

The Nothing's voice continued to resonate all over the entire world as he chuckled confidently at the King's response.

"You, Andreas of the House of Feather, are but one lone Archangel. I, on the other hand, am truly forever…I could shatter your feeble planet with one snap of my fingers. I could thrust your moon into the crust of your home and crush you all where you stand. I could bleed this world of its nourishing atmosphere and watch as you all burn into nothing!"

"Meet me on the Isle of the Sea Nymphs, Zealous," Andreas laughed, in response, "there will be no going anywhere for you if you do, in fact, destroy us all."

Andreas turned his gaze from the woodland and quickly made way for the island as it stood majestically in the clouds between the mountains.

Upon entering the stunningly tranquil gardens of the island, Andreas quickly noticed that all four of his daughters were standing still just before the waters that surrounded the giant and ancient stone archway that stood mightily in the centre of the Sea Nymph's lake.

"Black," the King gasped, "you should not be here right now…"

"No, father," she responded while closing over the grand bindings on the Book of Ancients, "this is exactly where I am supposed to be right now."

"Please, do not do this," he pleaded while running towards his daughters and the wood elf, as they stood together at the Sea Nymph's glistening lake.

"I am truly sorry, father," Black responded, "but White and I have both conjured up something immensely extraordinary."

"What do you mean?" he asked, The Nothing's voice continuing to echo and resonate throughout the waves of the air.

"We conjured together a prophecy for the most noble of hearts," White spoke, "and by using the Book of Ancients, we have bound the spell to ten of our most powerful Divine Artefacts."

Andreas kept his silver-white gaze trained on Black and let out a sigh of resignation and sorrow as his eyes slowly began to fill with the glowing tears of his angelic heartache.

"The spell will augment ten worthy humans from the young world of Earth," Black muttered as she wiped away her father's glistening tears, "and then when the time comes, the Warriors of Piathos will journey here to our world and restore all to which we have lost."

"I do not wish to lose any of you, my darling children," Andreas sobbed, tears running through his beard.

"You are all so very precious to me," he continued as he took his four daughters up in arms.

"How deeply touching this is…" The Nothing chuckled as he emerged into the tranquil greenery, which withered and died as he walked past.

The very image of The Nothing terrified the Sea Nymphs so much that they all lunged back under the waters of their magical lake in fear of his siphoning appetite.

Wisdom, too, froze up in terror as the enthralling perfection of The Nothing towered over everyone with just one simple smile.

"Do not be afraid, young wood elf," Zealous chuckled chillingly as he stepped towards the group in a dreamy haze of his clouding mist.

Black stepped boldly forward to meet The Nothing's gaze as the eldest Oracle nervously stationed herself between him and her family.

"Your sister too was frightened to face me," Zealous taunted as he gazed over at where White was standing. "You think that you have the power within you to stop me?" he continued to mock. "Living entities do not need our physical bodies as they are just a means for interaction. I am forever, and I am nothing to your feeble minds."

'O' shadow, eclipto, impenitri isolvox.'

Black slowly began to cast her chant.

"Go ahead, young goddess," The Nothing said with a coy and confident grin, "Infuse me with your utmost power…"

'O' shadow, eclipto, impenitri isolvox.'

Just then, the entire isle began to tremble and shake, as the lights of the luminescent plant life suddenly began to flicker and dim.

"Foolish tricks!" The Nothing laughed as he attempted to grab and throw Black out of his way.

As he began to push forward he stopped, confused. There was dark and still presence which barricaded Zealous from moving forward any further.

"If I am going down, Zealous, then you are coming with me," Black's expression tightened as the island continued to tremble and shake in the darkness of her overcast.

'O' shadow, round up The Nothing inside of yourself. Protect all those that it seeks out to poison. Shield it from the light of day and surround it in your endless sphere.'

"What are you doing?" The Nothing panicked as the darkness continued to slither and writhe like a serpent around him, "WITCH!"

'O' shadow, eclipto, impenitri isolvox.'

"Stop this now!" he barked in anger, "that is enough of your foolish trickery."

Black then gave a hubristic smile at The Nothing as she then proceeded to place her hands upon his panicked chest.

"I cannot breathe," Zealous exclaimed as he solemnly began to whimper and cry, "what kind of sorcery is this?"

Andreas and his daughters however, gazed on helplessly as Black suddenly began to drain The Nothing of all his power and all of his life force.

"This is it. It is now finally beginning to happen," Andreas spoke as Zealous slowly started to become frail and decay from being starved of all energy and life that was flowing from within and around him.

'O' shadow, eclipto, impenitri isolvox.'

And so, just then, the sphere of dark energy which contained the necrotized essence of The Nothing suddenly started to spin and twirl as Black masterfully began to craft it into a swirling typhoon of necrotic and shadowy energy.

Black turned her gaze towards the full moon as it gleamed brightly, high overhead. Her stunning blue eyes grew dark and just like a shadow they began to glaze over in a void of absolute darkness.

The twirling shadowy vortex of darkness was then hauled upwards into the night sky overhead with the utmost and immense force as Black proceeded to expel the unholy entity from their peaceful and sacred world. As the dark twister violently broke free out of the Piolan atmosphere, The Nothing was banished into the never-ending blackness of outer space.

"It is time to send me to the Earth," Black spoke with an ominous echoing tone as she turned to see her family.

"Now, before there is nothing left of me. I have made contact with The Nothing and I can feel his will beginning to fester atop my own," she said, tears rolling down her face.

Andreas then nodded his head and with the uttermost regret, he drew his Arcane Sword and waved its blade to open the gateway that sat unscathed upon the Sea Nymph's mystical lake.

"Follow the cosmic stream until you find the baby blue planet which chimes within the farthest galaxy. It circles around a young, golden-white star," the King muttered as he and his daughters watched Black do battle against the mist which lingered deep within her mind.

"I may find a way to return," Black muttered as she began to make her way across the garden.

"You must be ready for whatever darkness that I bring. I will not be the same sister that you see standing before you..." Black said as she made pace towards the mystical gateway, her very footsteps suddenly beginning to freeze the magical lake over in a layer of unkind and solid ice.

"I love you all dearly, please remember that," Black said as she took her final steps into the Sea Nymph's gateway, all of the light that once illuminated the mysterious island suddenly beginning to come aglow once more.

"What do we do now, father?" Green asked as she clung tightly onto Wisdom, tears stinging her face, causing plants to grow around the pair's feet.

"We rebuild..." the King muttered sadly in response, "things have now changed and the order of our world must change along with it."

"What do you mean, father?" Blue asked as she and White held tightly onto each other.

Andreas sheathed away his mighty Arcane Sword before turning his silver-blue eyes to that of his second eldest daughter.

"The City of Angels will need a powerful and kind-hearted new leader," he spoke.

"With The Nothing now free in the cosmos, it will only be a matter of time before he returns to the Celestial Realm with his dangerous and zealous followers. I have to go back to the Celestial Realm and warn my kin of this imposing threat. Please be strong and brave, my noble successors," his voice caught for a moment, "my darling daughters and most of all, the people's new champion, Queen White."

Wisdom dropped to one knee, his head bowed in reverence before the Oracle.

"Father, Black carries the Great Sight with her on her journey to Earth," White muttered in sorrow as she continued to embrace the King with loving arms. "I dare not think of what will happen to her if its holy powers decide to punish her for her noble and self-sacrificial deeds. This truly cannot be how her heroic story ends."

"No White, it is not," Andreas smiled as he wiped away the tears from her soft and gentle face. "Because of your spell in creating these saviours, the Warriors of Piathos will rise up from the Earth and chart a new era for all to see…"

And just as Black did mere moments before, Andreas walked the path across the frozen lake which thawed out as he stepped across. "Be good to each other, my beautiful girls. For this is not how the story ends…"

Warriors of Piathos

Chapter 1
Black as Night

*'For the Earth, may you bare the Warriors that destiny needs
and may you gift them with these Artefacts. Bind them to their
powers upon age through time and space.
Fire, tether with the quiver to find balance when calm collides
with chaos,
Water to the trident, so the soft can meet the current.'
'Lightning to this bracelet, may you conduct the will to control.
Plant life with the emerald, may the turmoil rest to tranquil.
Cryo to the sword, may the frost submerge with heat.
Serenity to this crown, may mind become the focus.
Mist to the snakes, may the cunning become the complete.'
'Great power and strength seal the belt.
Winds, bind the chains of this necklace piece, submerge the
sublime to flow with serene.
Energy, infuse these mighty gauntlets, and bring balance to
these beings blessed.'*

It was a clear and starry night in the sacred and mystical land of
Ancient Greece. And although it seemed to be calm and tranquil,
the young safe haven of Earth was soon to be struck down by the
first wave of tyranny and evil. And so, as the gods of the world
rallied together to find the Archangel Autt for safety and
sanctuary, Black the Piolan Oracle of night tarried alone in her
cavern which sparkled on the inside like the cold and distant stars
which graced the lonely cosmos above.

And as she pondered alone before her massive, black, boiling
cauldron, a tall, darkly hooded man soon entered into the mouth
of her small and intimate home.

"Are you the famed first-born Oracle from the far-off world
of Piathos?" The man asked as he then lowered the hood from
his robe to reveal his dark-skinned shaved head. "Allow me to

introduce myself. I am Prometheus, Titan of knowledge and the bringer of fire…"

"Yes, I know who you are," Black spoke as she turned to meet his gaze with a still and dry expression. "You come here to me because Autt has refused you and your family sanctuary for their misdeeds upon the lesser beings of mankind and their ilk."

"Please, you know as well as I do what evil awaits us all from beyond the stars," Prometheus muttered with desperation in his eyes. "The Nothing and his disgraced Celestials are coming…"

"So, for sanctuary from this damnation, you are willing to make a trade with me, is that correct?" Black smirked in response.

"Yes," he answered sharply. "Save my family, and I will give you whatever it is that your heart so truly desires."

"Be careful of what you ask of me…" Black spoke. "For what I ask of you in return is not something so easy to accept."

"Anything…" he muttered again. "Save my family."

Black then proceeded to smile at him as she took Prometheus' right arm in and pulled from her study a glistening, golden-and-red-jewelled dagger. "The weapon that I hold right here in my hand is a Celestial Artefact which once belonged to this world's monarch, King Autt."

"What are you doing?" Prometheus jittered in response.

"All Celestial Artefacts have the power to pierce the veil of immortality. But when combined with the correct spells, they can also strip those of magic free of their powers," Black said as she sliced the glistening blade along the Titan's right arm.

"What do you intend on taking from me?" he asked as she then turned to retrieve a small glass vial from the table which sat old and tattered beside her cauldron.

"Just a few drops of your divinity…" she said while cautiously collecting his godly, gleaming white blood inside of the small glass vial which she held carefully inside of her magic casting hands.

'O' shadow, celuni lio morbos don fort, magiria lio morbos, impiria, spirixo.'

And as Black commenced to cast her chant, the divine gleam of Prometheus' blood suddenly began to dissipate, and from his veins poured the red, hot, sticky substance of the mortals in mankind.

"Is that human blood?" the Titan exclaimed as he grimaced at his right arm.

"Of sort, I have now given your family sanctuary," she responded smugly as she sharply snapped her fingers. "Isn't that what you wanted?"

And from her quick finger click then came a sudden tremor which startled the ground beneath their feet. "What was that?" Prometheus gasped. "What did you do?"

"Fret not Prometheus." Black laughed mockingly at him. "For your family is perfectly safe... Under the graves of the people your entire empire had enslaved."

"What are you doing?" he grunted angrily at the Oracle as he grimaced again at her with a furious glare. "Trickery...? You strip me of my powers and then bury my castle under the valley it once proudly ruled upon."

"And in doing so, you and your petty family have now been saved from the flames of damnation," Black grinned. "Do not worry. You will get to keep your precious immortality."

"And what do you get out of all of this?" Prometheus yelped as he gazed over at Black who returned his gaze with a cold and dry glance.

"I get the last of the ingredients that I needed of course," she said while gazing longingly at the glowing white energy that was now safely contained within her small glass vial. "And what I really needed was to collect some of the most precious of magics from many of the Earth's most powerful gods. And all so that I could find and unearth the infamous legends itself, The Temple of Eternia."

"And why do you want to find the Temple of Eternia?" Prometheus asked. "Only the great King Autt can reveal such an immense an extraordinary sacred place."

Black then gazed up at Prometheus as she in turn exposed the crystal which sat gracefully upon her neck. "This here, my darling, is part of Celestial Artefact. It is in fact the last shard of the Great Sight and it has shown me the utmost of infinite knowledge and to that, the way back to my own home, my world of Piathos."

"And what shall become of me, my lady?" Prometheus asked as he then suddenly dropped tiredly to his knees.

"Ssh, you are going to be going on a very long journey, my child," Black smiled coyly as she spoke. "A journey of self-discovery and as the passage of time carries you through life on an endless voyage, you will then find the calling to which you were truly meant for."

Prometheus then tiredly shook his head as he slowly began to succumb to the power of Black's darkly magics.

"Oh, and one last thing," the Oracle spoke. "When the power of the prophecy that my sister and I had cast finally arrives and awakens the Warriors of Piathos, you will then in fact have the means necessary to regain the extraordinary abilities which I have just stripped you of."

And as Black mockingly laughed at him, Prometheus then finally commenced to fall under the thrall of her powerful and shadowy sleeping spell…

Chapter 2
The House of Feather

Thursday, July 17, 2008. Ithaca, Upstate New York.

It was yet another glorious summer morning in the beautifully preserved old town of Ithaca in Upstate New York.

"Hey Kenneth, happy birthday," Emma Feather exclaimed excitedly as she barged into her older brother's bedroom while he slumbered almost dormant under his double-sized, creamy-white duvet. "Uncle Andreas has a surprise for you downstairs."

Emma was a sweet and agile young girl who had the utmost stunning, long, red hair and aquatic-green eyes to compliment. She was always so full of energy and was too positive in contrast to her older brother, Kenneth Feather, who always felt somewhat more excluded from the world of mankind.

Kenneth then rolled over onto his left side with a tired yawning groan and said, "What is it Emma? Can't I go back to sleep for just a little while longer? That dream has been bothering me again, and I'm feeling a little blue."

"You always feel blue Kenneth," Emma chuckled as she stood tarrying at the edge his bedroom door. "Come on, you know that Uncle Andreas always talks about the contrast of your lonely daydreams and all the rest. But you are now seventeen and almost a man. So, I say that it's time to man up and get out of your bed!"

"Huh, are you serious…?" Kenneth groaned as he tossed his pillow at Emma before sitting up and shaking his head of thick, dark brown hair.

Kenneth was just like any other ordinary teenage boy at his age. He was a healthy young man that had the same drive as most, which was bedtime until noon. Unlike other teenagers, however, Kenneth had an extraordinary backstory which baffled even the most intelligent of minds. His eyes were very strange to stare at indeed, although it was mostly uncommon to have two completely different coloured eyes, be it brown and blue for instance. Kenneth, however, had the most obscure crossing of all. His left eye glistened with the utmost compelling gleam of ruby-red whereas his right eye was just a beautiful twinkle of ocean blue.

"So, I take it that the pillow coming, flying at me like a ninja on stealth signifies that your answer is a yes?" Emma chuckled playfully at her older brother as she launched the pillow back at his face.

"Emma…" he sighed with an expression of annoyance.

"Get up!" she exclaimed even louder.

"What is going on up there, Emma?" Andreas called up from the living room downstairs.

"Coming, Uncle Andreas," Kenneth exclaimed while jumping out of bed.

Meanwhile, some minutes later, Kenneth stepped foot into his en-suite shower where he then pondered deeply to himself upon the nightmare which had haunted him ever since he was just a child.

(Kenneth stood frantic and frozen in fear on the peak of a foreign mountain as a huge and ungodly hurricane stormed violently overhead. He was only a child at the time, not much older than six. And as the storm raged on angrily overhead, the young Kenneth could see what appeared to be a strange woman dressed in the most tranquil of heavenly white silk.

And as Kenneth peered ever closer to the perfection of the woman's image, he could see that the redheaded stranger was in fact unscathed by the chaos which whirled around her.

Then suddenly, Kenneth could hear the faint cry of a long lost yet familiar voice calling out to the blurred images that scurried frantically around him

"The Artefact!"

Kenneth then looked up again and saw that the serene woman was holding in her hands a pristine, red-jewelled amulet which she began to use in summoning the violent tempest from the cosmos above and beyond.

And as Kenneth gazed on, he could then see that the woman had grabbed hold of a man by the scruff of his neck. He was someone that Kenneth could not make out clearly however through the indistinct haze of his dreamy memory.

"Jane!"

The familiar voice echoed out once again. And then the sudden realisation of the name Jane quickly startled the young boy into an adrenaline fuelled charge to which he sharply called out...

"Mommy..."

Suddenly, Kenneth crashed violently into the woman as she tarried atop the mountain edge, which then caused the ruby-red jewel amulet to subsequently shatter all over his face upon impact...)

"Kenneth Feather, will you get down here!" Andreas angrily called out from the bottom of the staircase.

"Yeah, um sorry, I'll be down in a minute," he responded as he shook himself back into reality.

***

Ten minutes later, Kenneth had finally come downstairs to see his uncle and his sister sitting with two old, friendly faces which he had not seen since his early childhood.

"Aunt Lucy and Naomi..." the startled teenager exclaimed excitedly.

"Hey kiddo," their cousin Naomi smiled while embracing Kenneth in arms.

Naomi Sparks was the slightly older cousin of Kenneth and Emma. She was a very attractive young woman who liked to wear skin-tight clothes and leather jackets. She also often wore her long, dark hair back in a high-tied ponytail which exposed her sun-kissed completion. Her dark brown eyes were also highlighted by the sharpest of eyeliner although she did not overdo the use of her makeup.

"Where is Christian?" Kenneth asked as he next moved forward to hug his aunt.

"Oh, he's back at the Oasis with some friends," Lucy smiled as she stroked and squished Kenneth's stubbly face. "Oh, look at you both. You're both so grown up now."

Lucy was a small, petite and adorable round-shaped woman who was in her early forties. She had the sweetest of curly, cherry-red hair and the gentlest of green eyes. She wore on her head the fuzziest, red French beret and had the cosiest, fuzzy, red coat to match.

"Ah, damn, I was really hoping to see the little squirt." Kenneth said as he moved over to stand beside his great uncle.

"Don't worry, Kenneth," Andreas smiled. "You'll get to see him."

"Really," the teenager happily exclaimed. "That's awesome, so when does he get here?"

"No, he isn't coming here," Emma spoke while trying to contain her avidity. "We are going with Aunt Lucy and Naomi back to the Angelic Oasis…"

Kenneth then glanced back at his uncle who in turn smiled down at him in kind. Andreas was a kindly older man who always appeared to look grandeur and majestic in anything that he wore. His long, white beard and hair was always the image of tender perfection as were his eyes that glistened in the warmest of blue.

"Happy birthday, son," Andreas smiled softly again. "You better get upstairs and pack, your flight leaves at two and you won't arrive in the Oasis until 11 pm tonight."

"Wait, aren't you coming, Uncle Andreas?" Emma asked. "The Oasis is stunning, the last I remember of it anyway…"

"Unfortunately, I won't be coming with you," he responded. "You see, I actually have somewhere else that I have to be. And it has now come the time for me to leave here too."

"Wait, what?" Kenneth sighed as his heart suddenly began to sink. "I was really hoping for us to explore the town together there, you know just the two of us. Where will you be going?"

Andreas then took the kids up in arms as he spoke, "Do you remember all of those bedtime stories that I always used to tell you when you both first moved in here?"

"Yeah," Emma sighed as she happily snuggled into her uncle. "I loved the stories of how once a great King had a far-off magical land which he ruled gracefully over with his four magical daughters. And although he did love his Kingdom which was full of mystical beings, he knew that he had to leave when the time came for his magical princesses to come into their own destiny."

"And what did the King feel when this happened to him, do you remember?" Andreas asked as he continued to cuddle into Kenneth and Emma.

"He felt really hurt," Kenneth said as he smouldered in sadness. "But he had to go because his princesses had a greater responsibility and he, of course, had a new calling of his own, which was why it was the right time for him to leave."

"Yes," Andreas sighed. "And I wished that it wasn't the same for me this time round, but we now all have great new adventures to look forward to, right?"

"We will see you again, right?" Kenneth said as he smiled softly upon his great uncle's face whom he adored more than he could ever express. "Because the downside to your stories was that the Princesses never got to see their dad again."

"Of course, we will. We will all see each other again real soon," Andreas smiled. "I just have a few things that I need to address out of town. And you two, well, you're both going to get to begin your brand-new lives together with family and friends that you haven't seen in a long time."

"You promise, Uncle Andreas?" Emma chuckled.

"Cross my heart," he smiled in response before glancing up at Lucy who in turn gazed back at him with a more serious expression. "Um, why don't you guys show Naomi around while I have a little chat with your aunt?"

"Sure thing," Emma said as she planted a gentle kiss atop her great uncle's face.

"Oh and put something smart on you two," Andreas laughed. "We're going out for lunch, anywhere you want."

Chapter 3
Welcome to the Oasis

"Why did you take them Andreas?" Lucy asked all the while Andreas began to clear up his belongings. "After their parents died, it was down to me to look after them."

"They would not have been safe in the Angelic Oasis, Lucy." Andreas responded as his back remained turned from the angry petite woman. "Especially after the monstrosity of what had happened in Tanzania in 1996, after the dangerous Artefact that was uncovered by the archaeologists of Weatherfield Corporations, and after the unforgivable force of godly power that was almost unleashed upon this world. No, Lucy, they would not have been better off with you in the Oasis."

"Oh really," Lucy grunted while Andreas continued to clean. "Well then, you can at least look at me when I'm speaking to you."

Andreas then quickly turned his glance up towards Lucy as he gave her a long sigh before commencing. "It is their time to be with you now, Lucy. Your husband and your sister were not just the only two people that were lost to us during that time. My nephew, remember David, their father? He too was ripped away from us."

"So why now Andreas," Lucy asked. "Why now, after all these years of me searching and fighting for these two, why now do you finally yield and give them to me?"

"Because it is their time…" Andreas sighed with great sorrow in his heart. "I love those two as if they were my own and I would not trade a single thing in this world for those two and the precious memories that I have shared together with them over the last twelve years."

"But they are not yours, Andreas, they are my sister's and your nephew's children." Lucy answered. "So why do you leave now?"

Andreas then smiled up at Lucy as he wiped clear his misty-blue eyes. "Take care of them, Lucy. For this is how their story begins…"

***

And after saying their sad goodbyes at the terminal of Ithaca Tompkins Regional Airport, Andreas then proceeded to return to his big, wooden cabin by the quarry where he next unearthed his great and mighty Arcane Sword from the basement below the house. "Hello, old friend…" he sighed while glancing at the Artefact as it glistened and gleamed at the touch of his hands.

'O' Celestial forces here my call. Strip me of this mortal form.
Burn it down to ashes old and let me rise to be reborn.'

And as Andreas began to chant his holy spell, he was quickly ignited in Celestial flames which engulfed him of his human life. And after the ashes of his body fell, he was again born an Archangel once more.

And as the day of light had passed on, Kenneth, Emma, Lucy and Naomi finally arrived at the airport terminal of the stunning island, the Angelic Oasis.

***

The island was home to a ginormous pristine waterfall, a massive, natural, blue lagoon and many deep cave pools which sprouted out into streams and rivers that swirled all around the Oasis from the central aquatic reserve within Angel Falls Park.

"Hey Mom, Naomi, you're back and, yay! you brought my cousins too!" Christian Sparks exclaimed with excitement as Lucy went running happily towards him like a petite, fuzzy little, red charging rhino.

Christian Sparks was a very energetic, young, sixteen-year-old boy who was also very kind and gentle by nature. He had the most adorable of summer-blue eyes which too complimented his glorious, natural blonde, sun-kissed hair and his soft, white-freckled face.

"Christian," Lucy squealed as she smothered her young son in the arms of a motherly overload. "I trust you had a great day with Eric and his parents?"

"He was so very well behaved," Rebecca Tony spoke. She was a small, slender Japanese woman who stood at five-foot-tall along with the petite and fuzzy Lucy Sparks.

"Honestly Lucy, it was great to have him helping out around the house with us," Alan Tony said. He, on the other hand however, was a tall white man with a head of full dark hair.

"Mom, Dad," their son Eric smiled as Emma and Kenneth arrived at the doors with their bags in hand. "We should probably help these guys get back to Sparks Manor with their luggage."

"Yeah Mom, no need to worry…" Naomi muttered and groaned as she strained while dragging most of the suitcases along with Kenneth who was red-faced from carrying the weight of the bags. "Christian is not a baby, so he sure can help us haul all of this to the cars outside."

"Here, let me help," Eric spoke as he retrieved two large, black suitcases from Emma and Naomi.

Eris Tony was indeed a very attractive and slender, young, eighteen-year-old man of both Japanese and American features. He dressed, however, in the most pristine of clothing which appeared to be that of a male figure skater.

"Yeah Mommy, you're squishing me too much!" Christian muttered as he pulled away from Lucy's firm and loving grip.

"So sorry, baby," Lucy chuckled in response. "It has just been an entire day since I've last seen my beautiful boy's face…"

No more than an hour had passed before Lucy drove the teens in her little red car from the airport to their huge manor house which sat peacefully atop a grassy slope within the suburbs of the Oasis.

"Whoa," Kenneth sighed in awe as he and the others stepped out of the little red buggy. "The house is so grand… It's even more stunning than I can actually remember."

Kenneth continued to chuckle as he just couldn't seem to take his eyes off of the house as it gleamed in the glow of the pristine garden night lights which surrounded the manor on all angles from their garden.

"Oh, this is just little old home," Lucy giggled while Eric's parents pulled up behind them in the driveway.

"Well, that's the luggage here now, Mom," Naomi stated as the Tony's stepped out of their silver car to meet them on the lawn just before the house.

"So, it is," Lucy smiled. "Christian, sweetie, why don't you give a hand in helping me and the Tony's to bring the luggage into the house?"

"Sure thing," the young, blue-eyed blond sighed tiredly in response. "Naomi, want to give a hand?"

"Nah, I think that I'll just show these two around the house." Naomi responded sarcastically as she placed her right arm around Emma's shoulders.

"I'll give a hand," Kenneth said as he moved forward to assist his cousin with moving the bags into the house.

Sometime later after everyone had finished unloading and unpacking, Lucy quickly whipped up a nice pot of fluffy, hot coco for her and the four teens to enjoy before retiring off to their beds for the rest of the night.

"This house is stunning, Lucy," Emma smiled as the family sat around the dining table which sat in the open space between the kitchen and the living room.

"Thank you, my darling," Lucy responded as Naomi was the first to retreat off to bed. "You know the more I look at you, my dear, the more that I see your darling mother, my sweet little sister, Jane."

Emma smiled again before placing her empty mug down atop the beautifully varnished wooden table and said, "I must retire too, it has been an awfully long day of travelling and I think that some sleep will do me well. Goodnight, and thanks for the coco."

"Of course," Lucy sighed. "I hope that you like your new bedroom."

"Kenneth, I hope that you don't mind sharing with me." Christian said as he assisted his cousin up the stairs to their new bedroom which sat at the end of the hall. "I've always wanted to share a room," the blue-eyed blond chuckled.

"Interestingly enough, I've never really thought about it," Kenneth responded as he ascended the stairs to his new shared bedroom. "Although, I guess that your room is the biggest in the house so sharing it won't be all that bad."

"Yeah, Mom couldn't keep it after the accident in Tanzania," Christian said.

"Tanzania?" Kenneth asked as the pair made their way into the house's master bedroom. "I don't remember hearing anything about that."

"It's where your parents and my dad died," Christian responded with an expression of sadness. "But after the incident, you were the only person besides Joseph Weatherfield to return unscathed."

"Joseph?" Kenneth sighed.

"Max's dad," the young, blue-eyed blond yawned as he climbed under his silken-white bedsheets. "You'll get to meet them at the beach tomorrow. Anyway, let's get some sleep, I'm bagged…"

And as Kenneth slipped under his brand new, white duvet, he too began to doze off into the slumber of another nightmare-filled sleep.

Chapter 4
Meeting the Others

And so, as the sun shone brightly into the master bedroom of the Sparks Manor house the next morning, Kenneth quickly found himself waking up to the divine smell of pancakes, bacon and sweet breakfast waffles.

And upon opening his eyes however, Kenneth was quickly met with the stunning image of palm trees, clear blue skies and the ever-expanding waves of the distant Californian Sea.

"The Angelic Oasis..." he sighed while sitting forward to meet the town's gaze in all of its stunning and pristine glory.

"I don't want the goldfish to eat me..." Christian mumbled as he continued to snore in the bed which sat on the opposite end of the room.

Kenneth then shook his head at his little cousin as he commenced to giving a happy chuckle at the solace which he was feeling in that very moment. "Uncle Andreas, I wish that you were here to witness this."

Mere moments later, the bell chimed at the front door downstairs. "Naomi, that'll be the Blossomes, better let them come in." Lucy called out as Kenneth began to get changed into his blue denim jeans and white silken t-shirt.

"Mm smells good," Kenneth stated as he came stumbling down the stairs. "Hey, I was hoping that I could check in on my uncle later today, if that was okay?"

"Hey, you must be Kenneth," a blue-eyed, blonde girl stated as she sat next to Emma and Naomi at the dining table which was being served with all the glorious breakfasts imaginable. "I'm Sarah, Sarah Blossome, not Blossom, Blossome."

Kenneth then paused where he stood as he gazed upon the stunning young girl who was wearing the frilliest of summer dress of pink and white. "Uh, hi, hi, hey yeah, I'm Kenneth. It's nice to meet you Sarah Blossome not Blossom."

"Sarah has been filling me in on everything that we need to know about the school and all the rest," Emma said as Lucy and a handsome, young, Greco-Roman-looking boy emerged from the kitchen with more plates full of pancakes, toasts and other breakfast delights.

"Hey Kenneth, it's nice to meet you," the brown-eyed and deeply sun-kissed boy spoke. "I'm Paul, Paul Blossome."

"Not Blossom," Kenneth sniggered as he held his hand out to greet the young man in kind. "You guys siblings, huh? You both look so different."

"Yeah we're an interesting blend I should say," Paul chortled. "Our father was a Greek archaeologist and our mother is a Norwegian secretary."

"Right, although they were both born in the Oasis," Sarah smirked before a soft wave of sadness passed through her eyes. "Dad would have loved to gotten to meet you both all grown-up."

"Yeah, our parents all went to college together. They were all the best of friends," Paul stated as Emma and Naomi began to assist Lucy in bringing through the magnificent breakfast feast. "So it is really great that we finally get to meet you guys."

"Likewise," Kenneth smirked as Christian finally and tiredly came stumbling down the stairs and into the dining area where the masterpiece, which was breakfast, was at last served.

***

An hour after the majestic feast which was served up as a massive breakfast at the Sparks Manor had all but passed, and after the big clean up, everyone had begun to make their way to the west coast shore at the Angelic Oasis.

"So, what do you guys do for fun most Fridays around here then?" Kenneth asked as he and the Blossome siblings walked the town streets towards the beach where everyone would meet for Kenneth's surprise birthday party.

"We hang with our friends of course," Sarah smirked as she waved over across the road at a young couple who were walking on the opposite end of the street towards them.

"Who are they?" Kenneth asked as the young girl travelled across the street to meet the trio as they walked.

"Kenneth, we'd like you to meet our two friends, Claire Stevenson and Max Weatherfield," Paul spoke as the young girl excitedly ran into Sarah's arms, all the while the young guy happily strode towards them at an evenly and calm pace.

"Hey, you must be Lucy's nephew right," Claire chuckled as she playfully landed a punch on the young boy's arm. "I'm Claire, but enough about me let's talk, why is your left eye a ruby?"

"Whoa, easy Crazy Claire," Max chuckled nervously as he pulled the excitable young girl away from Kenneth. "We don't want to scare him off on his first official day here, now do we?"

"Don't worry about her, she's a harmless birdie," Sarah chucked at Kenneth as she and Claire linked each other in arms. "She's always gone wherever the wind carries her."

Claire Stevenson was indeed a very excitable young lady who had the most intense of curly brown hair and the most extreme, vibrantly big, blue eyes. She along with Sarah, Max and Kenneth were the only people among their friends group who were still only seventeen with Christian and Emma however still at the tender little age of sweet sixteen. Claire, similar to Naomi, liked to wear flexibly moving clothing. However, she was a little less profound and a little more relaxed in her choice of colour scheming.

Max, on the other hand, appeared before the rest of them dressed in the most expensive of summer gear. He had the most of a handsome-looking face with the smoothest tanned skin and mousy brown hair to compliment. And as he removed his rather expensive-looking sun glasses, Kenneth could see that the young Maximus Weatherfield had indeed the most compelling of emerald-green eyes.

"I don't usually say this, but you look good, man," Kenneth chortled as he held his hand out to greet Max where he stood.

"Likewise," the handsome, young man responded in kind. "It's really great that we finally get to meet you and your sister.

91

I was always so very curious to meet the boy that my father had saved all those years ago in Africa."

"I honestly don't remember that," Kenneth chuckled nervously in response. "Maybe you could tell me a little bit about it?"

"That's just the thing," Max sighed. "We don't actually know all of the details. It's just good to see that my father actually managed to save at least one life. The Oasis really suffered a big loss back in the nineties."

Claire Stevenson then proceeded to grab hold of Kenneth's right arm before pulling him forward towards herself and Sarah as to break the awkward silence of the mystery which was Africa 1996.

"So, we just met your sister Emma with Lucy and Naomi back at the grocery store," Claire spoke as the group continued to commence forward. "She's an adorable little redhead, what's she like?"

"Um, well she's a really active kid," Kenneth said. "She actually does gymnastics and she used to compete back at home when we lived with our great-uncle in Upstate New York."

"Really, that's fascinating," Claire continued as they walked. "So, tell me more about your ruby eyeball?"

"Um," Kenneth muttered as the group continued on along the sunny streets of the Oasis.

***

Sometime later, the rest of the group had finally caught up with the others at the west coast shore of the Angelic Oasis.

"Whoa," Kenneth gasped as he gazed around at the massive row of barbeques, bonfires and birthday gifts which Lucy and many of the other parents had prepared.

"Surprise…" Lucy giggled excitedly as Kenneth and the others had finally stepped foot onto the sunny, white, sandy shores of the west coast beach.

"This is incredible," Kenneth exclaimed. "Is Uncle Andreas coming?"

"Um, we'll talk about him later, sweetie," Lucy nervously chuckled as she handed over a box that was wrapped in the shiniest of blue wrapping paper. "Thank you all for bringing him here and for giving us time to prepare this wonderful party."

"Anytime," Sarah smiled softly as Emma waved her over from the shallows of the sea waves. "We should go and mingle, Paul. It looks like Eric and Josh have only just arrived too."

And as the Blossome siblings had parted along with Claire and Max, Kenneth then smiled awkwardly at Lucy as he asked, "Lucy, where is my uncle."

"Oh, um, he sent you this," Lucy chucked as she pointed at the box which Kenneth was now holding. "It arrived at the house for you just this morning."

"Thank you," he responded. "I really wanted him to be here today."

"I know," Lucy smirked as she kissed him top his forehead. "I'll just leave you to open it," she commenced before turning to re-join the many townsfolk who had turned up to celebrate at return of Lucy's long-lost family.

And upon opening his birthday gift, Kenneth was then met with a stunning portrait of himself when he was a child, his mother and a little, red curly-haired Emma. The portrait showed the family sitting together on a large rock at the west coast shore just by the Californian Sea. And as he gazed longingly at the picture, Kenneth began to shed a tear. For he could not remember his mother and he could not remember the life that he had lived before the mysterious accident which whisked him away from the Oasis mere months after the tragic loss of his beloved parents.

Then suddenly, from the back of the portrait fell a letter that was signed to none other than Kenneth Feather himself. Kenneth then wiped away his misty tears before retrieving the letter from the hot, dry sand and gazing longingly at the note as if it were some kind of foreign object.

Deciding not to open the letter right away however, Kenneth then placed the note into the back of his trouser pockets before shaking his head and commencing in an attempt to join in on the birthday celebratory activities.

"Your brother seems really nice, Emma," Joshua Stevenson stated as he and the others queued up in a line at the forest end of the beach for the delicious-smelling food which was sizzling atop the grill at the barbeque stands.

Josh Stevenson was a very tall and handsome yet goofy, slim built boy of seventeen. However, he was incredibly nerdy, as he wore on his face the most distinct of red-framed glasses which contrasted nicely with his smile which was a tad goofy but overall adorable. Josh also had the most unmistakable of shoulder-length, curly, brown hair which complimented his goofy yet adorable, glistening bright brown eyes.

"Why thank you, Joshua," Emma smiled as she, Josh and Eric all clamoured together around the grill where Josh's father and his uncle, who was his twin brother, stood guard over the goodies which were sizzling nicely atop the burning flames. "Although, he can be a little misplaced most days and so he is often my biggest mystery of life," she sighed as the trio watched Kenneth standing silently by the shimmering shores of the west coast beach.

And as the hours passed on into the shadows of nightfall, and the grills atop the barbeques became desolate empty, it was surely enough time to pack up and retire for the night.

"You know, despite my little quiet moment, I really did have a great time," Kenneth spoke as he, Emma, the Blossome siblings, the Sparks siblings, the Stevenson cousins, Eric and Max all sat together by the open fire which cracked into the last embers of its life.

"Yeah, me too Kenneth," Emma smirked as she gazed happily upon the portrait which their great-Uncle, Andreas, had sent over via airmail.

"We're all going back to the cars now, children. Are you all ready to leave?" Lucy called out as she gathered the last of Kenneth's birthday presents along with Paul and Sarah's little blonde-haired mother named Aavet Blossome.

Naomi then turned her head to her mother and gave a rather chilled-out sigh as she said, "It's all good, Mom, we'll all just walk back home together. Besides, it is a really stunning summer night after all."

"Okay, but be safe now, my lovelies…" Lucy chuckled before turning away with Aavet to leave the beach and return to their cars.

Then, suddenly from the darkness of the night came a face that was all too familiar to Naomi Sparks and the rest of the teens.

"Isn't it a little late for you kids to be hanging around the beach at this time on a Friday night?" a tall and well-dressed, bald, African-American man spoke as he walked the sands with a rather large, black-polished wooden cane in his hands. "I mean, even in the Oasis, strange oddities still may linger."

"Mr McKenzie, why are you out so late?" Naomi asked as the group turned to see the sharply dressed man standing tall before them.

"Always the sharp one, Naomi," the man chuckled as he gazed around to see both Emma and Kenneth sitting amongst the teenagers to whom he teaches at Cliffside High School.

"Cold as ice," Naomi retorted.

"Ha-ha," Mr McKenzie chuckled again. "So, there are ten of you now. Well, well, things are about to get interesting in the quaint little island town of the Angelic Oasis."

The ominous sound of the teacher's voice gave Kenneth the chills as he stood tall, dark and mysterious over the young teenagers who sat quietly before him.

"We'll see you on Monday, sir," Naomi finished as she waved the teacher off into the night.

"Yes, you will," he chortled lightly. "And it will be an honour getting to know you too, dear boy," he continued while gazing directly into Kenneth's soul. "Please, get home safely before the storm comes. This one has been long predicted from far and beyond…"

And just as quickly as he arrived, Mr McKenzie then vanished back into the shadow of the stunning summer night.

"Never mind him," Christian chuckled.

"Yeah he's a little too poetic," Paul stated. "Peter McKenzie, one of the smartest and wisest minds of Cliffside High. But also one of the most passionate, he's a great teacher despite his oddly rantings."

"Hmm," Kenneth sighed as he then returned his glance back to the shimmers of the clear and starry night sky.

Chapter 5
The Prophecy Manifested in Dreams

"Despite running into that crazy Mr McKenzie on the beach tonight, today has actually been one of the best birthdays that I can ever recall," Kenneth sighed as he and the other nine teenagers walked through the forest which was a shortcut between the west coast shore and the mainland park which was named Angel Falls. "I really do wish that my uncle had been here though."

"You really do love your uncle, huh," Eric said as the group walked along the brightly lit woodland pathway which led them directly towards the stunning greenery of Angel Falls Park.

"Trust me," Emma chucked, "Uncle Andreas and Kenneth were almost inseparable."

"Then why leave him?" Eric asked with an expression of curiosity.

"Actually," Naomi spoke, "Kenneth and Emma were supposed to come and live with us after mystery of Tanzania. But then Andreas came along and whisked them away from the Oasis. And up until recently, we had no idea what was going on."

"Naomi," Christian interrupted, "they were happy with their uncle and they were safe. That's all that matters."

"Sorry," Naomi sighed softly as she then gently patted Kenneth lightly on his back.

"I miss him," Kenneth muttered. "He is my absolute best friend. And I hope that one day he can come here and live with us together in the Angelic Oasis."

"It sounds like you truly do love each other," Sarah smiled while taking hold of Kenneth's right arm.

And so, just then from the sparkling nebula of the starry night sky, suddenly came a bright flash of Celestial light which was then quickly accompanied by a roaring, howling, whooshing

96

sound which swiftly pulled up a massive gust of rushing wind as it soared passed.

"What in the Oasis?" Claire Stevenson gasped as the gang was suddenly coated in a wave of stardust which was sprayed atop them like hot ash from the Celestial body which came whooshing through the Earth's atmosphere and briefly lighting up the night sky as it travelled.

And just as quickly as it came, the shooting star then ceased and the night sky became silent once more.

"We can all agree that that was weird, right?" Claire muttered as she and Josh shook their heads to clear their curly hair of the silvery glistening stardust.

"Yeah," Josh chuckled in response. "Sometimes it makes you wonder that Mr McKenzie might actually be some kind of soothsayer."

"Yeah, that was definitely weird, Claire," Kenneth said as he then proceeded to blow the dust free from his nose and mouth.

**

Sometime later back at the Sparks Manor, Kenneth Feather soon found himself sitting alone by the window atop the staircase just outside of bathroom where he pondered to himself as he gazed deeply upon the unopened letter which he held tightly in his hands.

"Hey Kenneth, are you okay?" asked Emma as she climbed the stairs from the bottom of the house.

He then turned to look at her before returning his gaze back to the unopened letter.

"Kenneth…?" Emma sighed as she placed her hand atop her brother's right shoulder.

"You know, Emma," he began, "the longer that I'm away from Uncle Andreas, the more alienated I begin to feel."

"Kenneth, is this about the letter that came out from behind the portrait?" the redheaded girl asked softly.

"I honestly don't know," he sighed in response before turning his gaze to the sparking night sky which glistened peacefully outside. "I mean I know that I have amnesia when it comes to our parents and our early life. And I mean, of course I can remember Lucy and the Oasis because we lived here before Uncle Andreas came along. But, he was always so good to us both and he gave us something that was so dearly precious."

"A good childhood," Emma responded. "Uncle Andreas always wanted what was best for the both of us in life. And now, this is the best for the both of us."

"But Emma," Kenneth sighed, "the further I am away from him pushes me farther from feeling like I don't fit in."

Emma then gazed at her brother with an expression of confounded bemusement as she quickly took the letter from Kenneth's hand and said, "I can't seem to understand how you still seem to feel this way Kenneth. But I guess opening this letter might give me some hints to what our uncle was always talking to you about."

"Emma, wait?" Kenneth mumbled as he snatched the letter back from her hands. "I'll open it now, all right."

"All right," she sighed in response while crossing over her arms. "Open it."

Taking a brief moment to compose himself, Kenneth then carefully opened up the note which was signed in black ink at the front and was addressed to **'Kenneth Feather'**.

(To my dearest Kenneth,
I know that this will be very hard for you to process, but things will not be returning to the way that they used to be. I am gone now and I will not be returning. Not in the way that you were hoping for at least.
I know that this is going to sound extraordinary, but you and your sister are the extraordinary. I had to remove you both from the Oasis for your own protection. If I had just left you both there, then you and all of your friends would have been in enormously grave danger.
For if you all had been marked as ten before the prophecy fell, then the followers of Zealous and other enemies alike would surely have found you.
Do not be alarmed by this my boy, for there are no words in the entire cosmos that could ever sum up my sublime love for you both.

Rest upon easy tides my child, for your life is now about to become an adventure that only few in man's world could simply ever dream of.
Love to you both, always.
Uncle Andreas.)

"So, what does it say then?" Emma asked as Kenneth drew in a long and sharp breath of air.

"I, um, I think that I just need to go to my bed," he said while folding the letter back into the open envelope. "Goodnight..." he continued while turning away to retire to the peace and quiet of his bedroom.

And as the young Kenneth once again fell into the slumber of yet another restless night, he soon found himself standing in a dream that was actually foreign to his usual puzzle of broken memories.

(Once again, Kenneth Feather soon found himself standing alone. However, there was no mountain or storm to follow, no blurry figures of people and no frightening yet beautiful woman before him.
***"What is this?"* Kenneth pondered as he soon realised that he was in fact standing on the woodland pathway walk that stood between the west coast shore and the massive greenery of Angel Falls Park.**
"Okay?" he muttered while gazing around at the dreamy haze of glowing mint green which was falling atop him like snow from the skies above.
And so, as Kenneth gazed up at the starry night sky, he could in fact see the asteroid which had showered everyone in a layer of silver stardust earlier that night.
And despite the slow-motion downpour of the luminescent stardust which trickled atop him from the skies above, Kenneth could see that everything else around him was actually suspended in motion.
***"Why is everything in slow motion?"* He pondered again as he then decided to follow the streak of light which was slowly gliding across that sky. And so, through the frozen woodland, Kenneth continued to walk until he reached**

the open beauty which was in fact the town's stunning landmark of Angel Falls Park.

"Can't get any weirder right? Or maybe I've just gone mad," he muttered again.

And so, Kenneth then proceeded forward into the lush greenery of the famous park which had seemed to be somewhat suspended in the natural flow of time as he walked.

Everything around him was absolutely suspended in a complete frame of stop-motion. All but the trickling drops of glowing dust and the streaking gleam of the Celestial light were completely halted as Kenneth continued to walk on forward through the park.

And as he passed through the giant waterfall which stood at the centre of the Oasis, Kenneth then found himself standing in a very ominous cemetery where he quickly spotted the glowing asteroid as it finally came to a halt upon grass before him…

"I should probably get my head checked," he spoke as he found himself studying the pulsing and radiant asteroid as it sat before an old gateway just beyond the graveyard. And upon closer inspection, Kenneth could see that it was in fact a rather stunning and exquisite golden-and-red-feathered quiver…)

"Whoa!" Kenneth exclaimed as he was then tossed out of his bed by the fast motion of suddenly waking up.

Oddly enough, the sound of Kenneth falling out of bed did not stir Christian as the young blonde just continued to snore into the fluff of his giant pillow.

And so, as Kenneth once again settled into the comfort of his cosy single bed, he was then startled by the words that were suddenly muttered aloud by his blonde-headed younger cousin as he slumbered peacefully in the bed opposite his own.

"The cemetery, just beyond the waterfall…"

Chapter 6
Tears of Flame

And so, yet another glorious morning returned to the Angelic Oasis as the bright and warm light of the sun broke free through the hills and the trees that inhabited life of the stunning aquatic island.

"Good morning, boys," Lucy spoke as she gently knocked on the outside of their bedroom door. "Kenneth, I think that you should come down here. I have some disconcerting news about your uncle, Andreas."

Suddenly waking to the name of his uncle, Kenneth then quickly lunged out of his bed and ran towards the door where his aunt stood nervously before him.

"I think that you should come downstairs," the small, redheaded woman muttered as Kenneth gazed at her with an expression of worry and concern.

***

Mere minutes later, the family were all stationed around the glass coffee table which sat elegantly in the perfection of Lucy Sparks' home.

"I, um, I really don't know how to explain this, but..." their aunt muttered as Kenneth and Emma sat on Lucy's large, fluffy, ocean-blue sofa next to their cousins, Christian and Naomi. "There was an accident. A fire, and your uncle, well, he couldn't escape."

Lucy then stepped aside to reveal a golden and black urn sitting lonely atop their homely fireplace.

"No, no, no. That can't be true, right?" Kenneth stuttered as he overtly gazed at his aunt for clarification of a different kind. And so, from the sudden shock, Kenneth's heart began to race uncontrollably inside of his chest as it then started to shatter and break, like an object of fragile glass. "This isn't true!" he roared before jumping up and running away. Back up into the sanctuary, his bedroom upstairs.

Emma, on the other hand, suddenly began to weep and cry as she then grasped tightly onto Naomi who in turn clung back onto her for comfort and support.

"I am so very sorry, my darling girl…" Lucy whispered as she and Naomi held onto Emma as she sobbed and cried into their arms on the couch.

"I'll go and see if Kenneth is okay," Christian spoke as he jumped up and followed his older cousin back into shelter, their shared bedroom atop the stairs.

And so, as Christian turned his gaze into the back of his bedroom, he was suddenly and quickly met with the image of his older cousin as he lay curled up and crying atop his bed. Wailing and whimpering, Kenneth clung tightly onto the note which he had just received from his great-uncle, only the day before.

"Hey buddy, can I get you anything?" Christian asked as he gently placed his left hand softly atop his cousin's back.

"I can't seem to make sense of this!" Kenneth wailed out as he suddenly lunged forward and pulled the note free from its envelope which his uncle had written just before his time of passing.

"Did he write something about it inside of the note?" Christian asked.

"I can't make sense of it…" Kenneth mumbled through hysterical cries. And as the tears of his grief ran free from his face and landed atop the note which he had held tightly in his hands, sparked suddenly something rather extraordinary and unexpectedly abrupt…

Unknown to Kenneth as he cried through grief, Christian quickly spotted that his big cousin's tears of sorrow suddenly began to ignite and burst into flames upon the moment they touched the paper which he held tightly in his hands. "Uh, Kenneth," the blue-eyed blond gasped as he swiftly lunged back.

Quickly spotting that his note was beginning to burn however, Kenneth then proceeded to douse the cinders that were suddenly starting to eat away the note which he had coveted most.

And as Christian too became startled by the scene of the flames which unexpectedly appeared on the note before him, the pair then suddenly noticed that all of the electrical currents in the house quickly began to exceed in power. And just as Christian turned around his hands, all of the lamps and light bulbs in their bedroom were suddenly defused and popped like balloons.

"Let me see that note, Kenneth," Christian mumbled as he quickly snatched up the letter from his heartbroken older cousin's hands.

Kenneth could then hear Christian mumbling the note aloud in the background as he turned his saddened gaze to the world outside of his bedroom window. And as he pondered in absolute despair, life in the Oasis outside seemed to commence on as any ordinary day would.

"Kenneth, I think that this letter is telling you more than you can actually see," Christian muttered softly. "It clearly states here that we would have been marked as ten and that would have drawn the followers of Zealous to us."

"My uncle always kept me grounded Christian," Kenneth whispered tiredly. "Without him I don't even feel like a complete human being."

"Dude, I'm pretty sure that you set this letter on fire. And I'm also fairly certain that I legit blew all of the electrics in this room…"

"I feel like I'm drifting away from humanity," Kenneth stated.

"Interesting, last night I dreamt that I was following the shooting star along the pathway between the park and the bay, and it lead me right to the old cemetery just behind the great waterfall."

"What?" Kenneth asked as he quickly snapped himself back into concentration. "I dreamt that too."

"Nice," Christian responded calmly. "Let's just keep an eye on everyone else who was with us that night. I mean, who knows, they may have developed strange abilities too, right?"

"I can't seem to process anything right now," Kenneth tiredly yawned in response.

"You're in shock Kenneth," Christian said. "Go for a nap now, and then we can think this through after the weekend is over."

Kenneth tiredly nodded his head in agreement as he then proceeded to lie down before closing his misty and red sore eyes.

Chapter 7
Strange Happenings

Monday, 27, July 2008.

And yet another glorious dawn suddenly began to bloom upon the aquatic island of the Angelic Oasis. And though it was once again a very vibrant morning, Kenneth still found himself reeling from the loss of his one true friend all the while pondering upon the note which gave him some fragments of hope.

"Now that we've got you both signed up for school, I think it's time that we get you settled into everyday life on our quaint island out here in the Oasis," Lucy chuckled as she dropped off her four precious gems at the front entrance of Cliffside High School. "Oh, and after your first day here, I was thinking that we could go somewhere and scatter your uncle's ashes. Or we could even keep them and say a prayer for him over a lovely, family, home-cooked meal together."

"That would be really great," Emma sighed while smiling at her aunt through the reflection of the rear-view mirror, "thank you, Lucy."

Kenneth, on the other hand, did not respond as he continued to study his uncle's letter which was cindered and burned from the unexpected pyrokinetic teardrops that he had cried upon the note, just the other night before.

"Kenneth," Christian grunted under his voice as he gently nudged his older cousin lightly on the left-hand side of his ribs.

"Yeah, of course," the teenager responded, "thanks for everything, Lucy, and sorry for being so emo."

"It's quite all right," Lucy said, as many students and teachers alike all piled into the giant school grounds from the yard just outside. "Naomi will keep you company here, Kenneth.

Most of you are in the twelfth grade anyway. So, it's not like you'll be alone or anything."

"I'll look after Emma, Mom," Christian said as they then exited the little red car.

"Have a great first day kids," Lucy called out, as she then once again started up the engine of her tiny little red vehicle. "See you all at four…"

***

Sometime later around 11 am, Kenneth soon found himself sitting with Naomi and Eric at the front desk of none other than the passionately poetic teacher of world History, Mr Peter McKenzie himself.

"This guy really intrigues me…" Kenneth muttered quietly to Naomi as the students all settled into their seats within the history class.

"He is somewhat eccentric…" Naomi responded in kind.

"Yes, Miss Sparks," the teacher retorted loudly, "always the sharp one you are, as cold as ice you said. And eccentric indeed, I am. Turn to page ten please."

Naomi then grinned cockily over at him, before grimacing behind his back with a very cold and unkind expression of bemusement.

And then, suddenly, from Naomi's hands came a very obscure ray of frost which crystallised atop her desk and shattered the black ink pen that she was holding onto in her right hand.

None of the other students however noticed the layer of ice which had oddly appeared beneath Naomi Sparks' hands. And although the exploding pen did seem to catch much unwanted attention from the teenagers, they still remained oblivious to the cryokinetic ability that was just displayed by the school's very own Queen of ice, Naomi Sparks herself.

Yet, it was only Kenneth and Eric that had spotted the frost however. And although, Kenneth did not seem too startled by what he had just seen, Eric and Naomi on the other hand, were at a complete loss for vocal words.

"Incredible," Kenneth sighed as he then gazed at his cousin who was quickly wiping herself clean of the ink which had splattered atop her from the shattering of her nice, silver-laced pen.

"No need to be alarmed kids," Mr McKenzie spoke, as he then opened up the history textbook which he held atop his teaching desk. "Everyone, please turn to page ten in the history book of Ancient Greece."

Suddenly and uncontrollably, Kenneth could then feel a strange warming sensation rushing all the way through his body as he focused sharply onto the book which sat open upon Mr McKenzie's desk. And just like before, the pages that lay open from within the book of history quickly began to smoulder and burn as the paper within the textbook rapidly burst up into a blaze of glorified fire.

Not looking too startled in the slightest, Mr McKenzie quickly gave a brief, ominous glance at Kenneth and Naomi before jumping up and tossing the book into the trashcan and then dousing it with the coffee from his giant, silver flask.

"Well then. I think that's enough excitement for one day," Mr McKenzie muttered and coughed, as the black smoke from the flames swirled and swooped into the air just above the teacher's head. "Everyone, turn to page ten please."

And from that moment on, everything within Kenneth's being now knew that there was something more to their history teacher than just that of his ramblings and poetic passions.

***

Later on that evening, around 8 pm, and after the wonderful family meal that Lucy had prepared in honour of Kenneth and Emma's dearly departed uncle had all but ended. Kenneth and the others had then decided to congregate together at the house to discuss the note which Andreas had left for him and the oddity of the strange and wondrous happenings that were occurring.

And so, Kenneth had then also decided to round up his friends into the living room of their home when Lucy had taken off to attend a late-night meeting at her place of work, which was in fact within the majestic halls of Weatherfield Corporation.

"That's twice now," Kenneth spoke as the ten teens gathered together within Lucy's pristine and perfect little lounge room. "Me, I'm setting things on fire with my mind. You, Christian, you seem to be channelling electrical currents of some sort. And Naomi, you actually made ice come out of your hands... What about the rest of you guys, have you all been effected too?"

"This is insane, Kenneth," Emma sighed as she shook her head in disbelief, "I honestly don't know what on earth you are talking about?"

And so, just then, as Emma was venting, all of the water that was sitting contently within the mop bucket behind the group suddenly exploded and ruptured upwards into a gigantic aquatic water plume.

"Not again," Emma sighed, as the water then splashed all over the kitchen floor behind her, "there is obviously something wrong with the water pressure."

"In a mop bucket, there are no pipes in there Emma!" Christian exclaimed.

"Now Emma, listen to me okay," Kenneth spoke, as Sarah and Paul sat quietly beside him on the sofa. "I think that we all have powers now. And I think that Uncle Andreas was trying to tell me about it in the letter that he sent me."

"What?" Emma laughed nervously in response, "You, my brother, are completely crazy!"

"Emma, please," Kenneth sighed, "read the damn letter."

In complete shock, Emma's face then quickly began to turn white as she read the note aloud to everyone all the while they sat and focused on the words that the redheaded girl had spoken. "You've turned me into some kind of freak?" she yelped hysterically.

"Emma. Did you, like everyone else here, share the same dream about that asteroid that we all saw from the night before?" Kenneth asked while he then reclaimed the cindered note which his redheaded sister waved around frantically as if it were a white flag.

"I don't pay much attention to my dreams, Kenneth. But, I actually did dream about following that comet through the park and into a strange, creepy cemetery place. What have you done to me?" Emma then exclaimed abruptly in anger.

"Has anyone else displayed an oddity of any kind?" Christian asked, as he then gazed sharply around at everyone who was sitting quietly within the room.

Sarah Blossome then raised her left hand and with one simple pulling motion she suddenly moved one of Lucy's wooden chairs away from the table as it sat quaintly within the Sparks' dining room area.

"I started to display a telekinetic ability earlier this morning when I heard our mother yelling at Paul to get up out of bed," the young, blonde and blue-eyed girl muttered. "To be perfectly honest, I didn't think too much of it and I was actually kind of hoping that something like this would happen, especially after that downpour of cosmic dust."

"Look, I really have to admit," Eric Tony muttered. "This is strange. And I think that these powers are manifesting from our heightened states of emotion," he spoke calmly as he then stood up from the arm chair that sat quaintly just beside Lucy's fireplace. "To be honest, during skating practice after class and miraculously witnessing Naomi getting frosty, I suddenly realised that I was being surrounded by a strange fog while dancing on the ice. And then I noticed that everyone else that was around me was suddenly suspended in a strange sleep like stasis."

"Well, I don't know about you guys," Claire Stevenson exclaimed excitedly, "but I think that we should all go to the park and find out exactly what's been happening to us."

"What's that?" Josh asked as suddenly an immense gust of cold wind swiftly blew through the house which then knocked over many of Lucy's precious and well-collected ornaments and her rather expensive and well-kept furniture.

"Figures, you'd get aerokinesis, Claire," Paul Blossome chuckled, "I just got your everyday garden variety of power. I can manipulate the motion of plants. It happened not too long after you called."

"Whoa…! Now that's what I call, titty power!" Claire chucked as she shook her head of big, air-blown, fuzzy, brown hair, "I was hoping that I'd get something really wild like the wind."

Emma's face then turned even whiter than previously expressed as she drew in a deep breath and yelled rather loudly, "Titty power…?"

"Coincidence, I think not?" Kenneth answered confidently, "I don't actually believe that our uncle is really dead."

"Coincidence or not Kenneth, we will not be leaving these premises until we have cleaned up the entirety of this god-forsaken mess!" Emma yelled, as Kenneth and Christian cheered happily together.

"Oh, yeah Mom will not be pleased to see her house in disarray when she gets home from the office," Naomi stated, as she patted the boys playfully upon their backs. "So, then we should probably get busy and clean all of this before mother dearest returns and transforms into the dreaded Crazy Poppins."

Christian then quickly sprung himself into the kitchen and grabbed hold of the mop before calling out to everyone else who was all sitting quietly within the Sparks Manor living room. "What are you all waiting for? If my mom sees this mess, then it is going to be far worse than the actual apocalypse…"

Chapter 8
Messengers of The Nothing

No more than an hour had passed on before the group of ten had left the now sparkling clean home of Sparks Manor before venturing off out into the large greenery of Angel Falls Park.

"So, you're hoping that we find something useful out here?" Paul asked Christian as the group soon travelled on by, passing the glistening lakes and streams that flowed through the park like an open aquarium of lush heavenly beauty. "Because I'm starting to worry about the part on the note that states that we are literally targets for crazy zealots of some kind."

Christian then turned to his friend and grinned coyly before stating, "Don't you worry about a thing, we are all here together and to top it off we actually have real superhero powers. So, we'll be fine."

"Thanks for the vote of confidence, blondie," Paul chuckled nervously in response, as the group then ventured on by the open pond which was illuminated in the gleam of lanterns and garden night lights.

"Rather ominous, isn't it?" Kenneth muttered as he pointed over to an old run-down church which sat almost in ruins by the pathway leading up to the stunning waterfall which sat gracefully overhead.

"Oh, yeah that place has seen better days," Sarah answered. "It's the old cathedral that used to house the Oasis nuns back in the eighties. But, then it got shut down for refurbishment almost two decades ago. And it hasn't been open since."

Just then however, a strange green luminescent glow suddenly appeared from the inside of the church as the teenagers quietly walked on by.

"That's odd..." Kenneth sighed.

"Guys," Paul muttered under his breath to the group as they continued to move forward along the woodland walkway. "Look around you."

Suddenly and to the group's surprise, the entire park had now become overrun with a ton of nuns that were peacefully pacing around the grounds with green-lit lanterns in their hands as they commenced to walk together in prayer.

"Maybe they have just come back?" Kenneth chuckled nervously. "Total coincidence?"

"I don't like this," Paul muttered anxiously. "Something isn't right here."

"We have to get out of sight," Naomi stated as she urged the rest of the team to proceed forward away from the public's gaze. "Let's get out of the public's eye."

"Naomi," Paul exclaimed again under his voice. "What if that's what they want us to do?"

"Then they got a fight on their hands..." she responded briskly.

**

Only several minutes later as the team had then dispersed away from the view of all the nightly dog walkers did they finally notice that the ominous glow of green light was slowly but surely following on behind.

"They are gaining on us," Emma winced as suddenly a great flume of water was plumed up out of the waterfall's lake and splashed all over the team as they travelled.

"Calm down, Emma," Naomi spoke while edging the team to commence forward. "It could be nothing..."

And so just then, a huge team of nuns suddenly came walking around the corner of the pathway while chanting together in an oddly ancient language. Their faces remained concealed however and only became revealed once they began to jeer in unison the dreaded name which the letter had stated very ominously.

'Zealous, Zealous, Zealous...'

The chanting continued as they gained upon the group of ten with cold eyes of darkly horror.

"Does anyone else know how to use their powers yet?" Kenneth exclaimed in panic as suddenly many of the lanterns which they held in their hands exploded outwards into a huge outburst of debris and flames.

To the group's surprise however, the nuns commenced forward with their chant despite the burning flames which appeared to have no effect upon them as they continued to chant,

'Zealous, Zealous, Zealous...'

"We're done for..." Claire yelled as suddenly a powerful gust of wind picked up and blew a massive ton of water up out from the graceful waterfall.

"Run!" Naomi exclaimed. "Get to the cemetery."

And as the group proceeded to run through the walkway that stood just behind the huge falls, Naomi suddenly began to focus hard upon the water that was sprayed outward from the winds that swept wildly all around them.

And so, just then, from the downpour of the sudden gust came a swift hailstorm of sharp spikes and heavy frozen icy debris.

"That'll sure keep them busy?" the dark-haired girl chuckled before turning away to join the others as they ran towards the cemetery grounds.

Chapter 9
The Cemetery

"Brace yourselves!" Christian yelled while his big sister quickly came running to meet the others as they waited for something to happen upon the Angelic Oasis burial grounds.

"I can only see some scorch marks just there before the old gateway," Kenneth exclaimed as the team of nuns suddenly came at them from beyond the falls in numbers that were just far too many. "Look out!" he cried.

"Whoa!" Paul yelped as he accidentally summoned a growth of roots to bind and restrain the fiendish, frightening nuns as they charged.

But despite holding back only a few of the antagonistic foes, many of the others rampaged upon them like a sea of black cloth.

And so, into combat Naomi and Josh quickly commenced.

"I didn't know that Naomi could fight?" Kenneth yelped as he swiftly avoided the shadowy blades of the ominous and darkly nuns.

Using her athleticism, Emma Feather then quickly sprung out of the way while adding kicks and evasive manoeuvres into the routine of her gymnastics dancing.

"I have super-strength!" Josh chucked as he easily tossed aside the cackling nuns like toys, as they came at him with their darkly and ceremoniously formidable-looking blades.

"That's fantastic, but how do we stop them?" Max asked as he lunged forward both of his hands so to cause an explosion of molecular energy. "Oh crap, my powers are just the worst."

And just as Max swatted forward both of his arms, the nuns that came at him were quickly shattered from limb to limb.

'Zealous, Zealous, Zealous...'

The nuns continued to chant. All the while, their bodies began to become distorted and twisted as suddenly they regenerated and reformed from the energy of the explosion.

"Oh, that is so not good?" Max gasped as the nuns then began to corner the teens into one small segment of the cemetery grounds...

Chapter 10
The Celestial Being

And just then, suddenly, from the old gateway, came an incredible beam of unfathomable and warming white light which illuminated the entire park like an intense gleam of otherworldly energy.

"What…?" Kenneth exclaimed as the nuns suddenly began to cower and weep in a waving sweep of paralysing fear.

'O' Celestial forces, hear my call. Cleanse these grounds of unholy thorns.'

Screaming in writhing agony, the formidable army of ungodly nuns quickly then began to burst into Celestial flames where they stood. Leaving behind in their wake merely a dust cloud of ash that was soon carried off into the cool evening breeze of the night.

"Never let those shades near you," a friendly male voice spoke as the flash of incredible light soon wilted away into the calm and collective glow of yet another stunning summer night. "They are tainted in the darkest of evil and have the utmost, immense and formidable of power."

As Kenneth and the others soon stood to greet their rescuer in person, the team were suddenly met with the most stunning of Celestial images. "Who are you?" he asked curiously.

"My name is David," he spoke while standing firmly amid a warming glow of Celestial light. "You should all come into my domain. Your Divine Artefacts have now arrived."

David was the watchful protector of the Warriors of Piathos and a Guardian Angel, who resided deep within a pocket realm that was allocated just behind the cemetery at Angel Falls Park.

Although his physical appearance emerged in a younger form of mid to late twenties, he was actually, in fact, over twelve thousand years old.

And as David stood mightily before the teens, he held firmly in his hands a Celestial weapon which was indeed a tall, white and golden Trident that stood at height with his complete Celestial form which was approximately eleven foot tall. He also had the most hypnotic and compelling, dazzling, moonlight-blue eyes that along with his draping, silken, long, white-blonde hair made him appear even more dazzling than any human possible.

His armour too was of a shining and shimmering Celestial metal which actually appeared to reflect that of a stunning summer day sky even though the stars above them shone brightly overhead at night.

Turning around to the gates again, David commenced away from the cemetery as he magically folded in his six majestic wings that miraculously vanished from his back as they were elegantly curled into rest.

"That dream of the meteor. It leads you here to this place," David spoke softly. "Come with me to my domain, and I will show you all how to best protect yourselves. Or stay out here and wait for the Dark Priests return in kind."

Despite his oddly approach however, the group of ten teenagers decided to follow the angel as he suddenly vanished from sight like a glowing candle through the arch of the unlocked gateway as it sat open at the end of the Oasis burial grounds.

"Not ominous at all…" Paul Blossome chuckled as the team vanished through the gates just behind him…

And as they passed through the gates, the team then suddenly found themselves standing in the most dreamlike of gardens which sat heavenly surrounded by blue-lit skies before an incredibly large and white-stoned mansion. *So, this is what happens beyond the dream?* Kenneth pondered as the group continued on just behind the Celestial Being.

"So beautiful," Sarah gasped in awe as the teenagers all gazed around wide-eyed at the pristine beauty which surrounded them in kind.

And so, melted away the darkness of the outside world, and to the teens' understanding suddenly came the realisation of pure Celestial bliss. And from the great light swiftly came the bright blue sky revealing beautiful green meadows, crystal clear lakes and plant life so rich that could only ever be seen through the eyes of an innocent's dream.

"Welcome to Angel Falls," David smiled as he then opened up the huge, white doors of the mansion that stood grandly in the glow of the realm before them.

"My, my, my," Naomi sighed as the teens entered into the grandeur halls of the Angel Falls Celestial Realm's hidden home.

And so, as they continued to walk through the house, Kenneth noticed that the walls within the corridors of the mansion were graced magnificently with the many portraits of Guardian Angels and Archangels alike.

"Please come, eat and rest. For now, you are all safe. And we indeed have so much here to discuss," David spoke as he opened up another set of massive doors that lead right into the great mansion's lounge room.

"Kenneth," Emma exclaimed as one specific portrait that sat just above an open fireplace suddenly jumped out to meet her attention. "That angel in the painting, he looks just like. No. It can't be? Uncle Andreas…"

Chapter 11
Bonding with the Artefacts

"Ah, yes," David spoke as the little old man, his servant, trotted through…trotted through into the lounge with a silver tray of home-baked goodies. "That Archangel there is Andreas. The King of all Piathos…"

"Mind blown…" Christian chuckled as he patted a very much gobsmacked Kenneth atop his back. "What are the chances of that happening, Kenneth?"

"Oh yeah, that's Andreas all right," Naomi gasped in response. "Only met him a week ago and there is no chance of mistaking that face."

"Many things happen in this vast universe," David muttered. "Andreas was also the father of…"

"His four magical princesses," Emma interrupted. "The King had to leave their sacred home because it was his daughters' time."

"Yes," David smiled softly as he sat down upon a rather comfy and cosy white armchair. "And now, you see he actually had a greater purpose for leaving. If not for his return to the Celestial Realm then The Nothing would have surely conquered many other unexpected and innocent worlds. And, of course, his eldest daughter was indeed tainted by absolute darkness from using her own powers to drain The Nothing of his."

"Ooh, then what happened?" engrossed by the story, Claire clasped her hands together before nodding at him with an expression of intrigue.

"You are the Warrior of Air," David chuckled as he gazed curiously upon her. "I can tell because your nature goes to wherever the wind takes you."

"David," Kenneth sighed. "David was my father's name, did you know that? So David, please tell me why my uncle's portrait hangs upon your hallowed walls."

Giving a slight grin of respect to the young boy, David then stood from his seat and waved his trident at another doorway which swung open upon his command.

"Andreas was ordered to protect the Warriors of Piathos before the time and coming of their powers," the Celestial being spoke. "Your powers, you see. And in doing so, he has now fulfilled his scared duty. So at last, back home he has been summoned upon where he may rest and recharge into his once and true form."

A tear then rolled by Kenneth's face as he once again felt his heart begin to shatter and break inside of his chest. "So we meant nothing to him?" he spoke through a broken tone.

"No," David answered softly. "You meant everything to him. And leaving you, son, was the hardest thing that he could ever do." The young Celestial being then turned his gaze to Emma as he once again continued to speak, "You too girl, I know that your uncle gave you both an amazing life with incredible memories of love and happiness."

Emma then gave a soft smile as she, too, let loose a few tears of heartbreak and sorrow.

"Please, blessed Warriors of Piathos," David continued, "allow my friend Billy here to show you into the armoury where your destiny awaits. It is now time for you all to become bonded with your own Divine Artefacts."

The little old caretaker of the grounds named Billy, quickly guided the young teenagers into a large room that was stock-piled with magnificent trinkets and objects of all kinds.

"The Artefacts that had fallen from the heavens above have now been collected and placed within this room." The four-foot-ten, grey-headed man muttered as he waddled around like a cute, silver, teddy bear.

Commencing on with the story however, David began to explain the ritual of the Oracles which created the Warriors and bound them to their powers.

*'For the Earth, may you bare the Warriors that destiny needs
and may you gift them with these Artefacts. Bind them to their
powers upon age through time and space.
Fire, tether with the quiver to find balance when calm collides
with chaos,
Water to the trident, so the soft can meet the current.'*

David spoke as one by one the teenagers soon found their
respective Artefact, as they lay scattered around among the
stands.

*'Lightning to this bracelet, may you conduct the will to control.
Plant life with the emerald, may the turmoil rest to tranquil.
Cryo to the sword, may the frost submerge with heat.
Serenity to this crown, may mind become the focus.
Mist to the snakes, may the cunning become the complete.'*

*'Great power and strength seal the belt.
Winds, bind the chains of this necklace piece, submerge the
sublime to flow with serene.
Energy, infuse these mighty gauntlets and bring balance to
these beings blessed.'*

"A girl sure knows her accessories," Sarah chucked as she
placed a clear-jewelled tiara atop her soft, blonde head. "Whoa,
that feeling..." she gasped in awe. "It feels like..."

"It was made just for you," David smiled. "Sarah Blossome,
you are indeed the Piolan Warrior of the Mind. And so, your
powers reside within your very thoughts."

"Hey, I got this really beautiful emerald headpiece," Paul
muttered as he too placed the jewelled object atop his head.
"Don't judge me guys, this is one sweet, glowing, green bling."

"You, Paul Blossome, are the Piolan Warrior of Plant life.
And so, you indeed hold domain over the plants of this Earth,"
David spoke as he smiled proudly upon him.

The Stevenson cousins then pulled from the archives their
respective Artefacts of a white-feathered necklace for Claire and
a black-leathered belt with a ruby button and dark, coating fur
for Josh.

"You, Claire Stevenson, are, as I stated before, the Piolan Warrior of Air. And you, Joshua, are indeed the Piolan Warrior of Strength," David smiled proudly again.

"It's funny," Naomi stated as she then unsheathed a great glacier sword of steel. "You see, we all dreamt of finding these objects in the cemetery on the very same night that we were miraculously showered by a cloud of cosmic stardust."

"The glacier-steel sword," David spoke as he then turned his gaze to that of Naomi as she stood with the blade firmly in her hands. "You, Naomi Sparks, are indeed the Piolan Warrior of Ice."

"Naturally…" the dark-haired girl smirked coyly.

"Why does she get a sweet ass sword?" Christian muttered as he stepped out from the archives amongst the scattered Artefacts. "Not that I'm actually complaining because I just found this sweet ass clear-jewelled bracelet that I had been dreaming of, sweet or what?"

"Because you, Christian Sparks, are indeed the Piolan Warrior of Electricity, and that bracelet will help you to conduct the will to control," David smirked before turning to gaze at Eric and Max as they stood amongst the library of objects.

"These earpieces are so very beautiful," Eric sighed as he held in his hands a stunning set of silver, snake-figured duel ear jewels which he gazed upon with endless longing. "They look like something that I could only ever dream of. Indeed, they would match any outfit that I would wear for my skating, of course."

"You, Eric Tony, you are indeed the Piolan Warrior of Mist. And so, your power resides in the density of the atmosphere," David smiled again.

And so, as Max Weatherfield stood idly by an altar amongst the archives, he soon became frozen in sheer awe by an extraordinary set of silvery gleaming gauntlets that sat almost immediately before him on a stand amongst the objects.

"Take them, Max, they belong to you," David sighed softly. "You are indeed the Piolan Warrior of Energy and your powers reside in molecular motion."

And lastly, the Celestial being turned his gaze overtly towards that of the young Feather siblings who were standing mere inches from their respective Piolan blessings of Artefacts.

"You, Emma Feather, are indeed the Piolan Warrior of Water," David smiled immensely at the young redhead as she stood mesmerised before him with her glowing-blue trident firmly in hand. "Your powers reside in and all of the water that lives in and around you, my child."

And so, as David turned his attention to Kenneth, he swiftly and softly spoke while gazing deeply into the young man's ruby-red eye. All the while Kenneth, on the other hand, held in his hands the red-feathered quiver which he had seen in the dream that had but only once blessed him free of his tortured and broken memory.

"You, Kenneth Feather, are indeed the Piolan Warrior of Fire," he spoke as he continued to gaze down upon the now appointed Warriors of Piathos. "These Artefacts will insure that you will all in time gain full control of your newfound powers."

"How do we use them?" Naomi Sparks then asked rather briskly. "I mean I can't be seen strutting around the Oasis with a giant ass glacier-steel sword."

"From the moment that these Artefacts passed on through the Earth's atmosphere, they had then showered upon you with the residue of their sacred and magical properties. And in doing so, they correctly melded their enchantment to the very DNA of each and every one of you," David swiftly and suddenly began to explain.

"How does that explain the sword carrying?" Naomi asked briskly once again.

"From the very moment that the debris of the shower had touched you, the magics of the Oracles spell had begun to connect you directly to these Artefact," David spoke. "So, you can actually hide them from sight if you really so wish it."

"I so wish it," Naomi muttered as she accidently condensed the size of her brand-new sword into that of a small and easily portable pocket keyring. "Well that's neat…"

"I had indeed enchanted these Artefacts separately to cater to your needs within the world of mankind which resides just beyond on the outside. Be well my Warriors for I look forward to seeing you all again," David smiled before waving his trident around and sending the Warriors back to the battleground of the Oasis cemetery outside.

Mere moments after David had sent the Warriors back into the realm of man's world outside, the Celestial Being was then met with a kindly, familiar and friendly old face. "You had raised them well Uncle," the blue-eyed blond muttered.

"Of course, I did," the voice of Andreas spoke as he emerged into the grandeur halls of the Angel Falls armoury. "Thank you for allowing me to love them all these blessed years, David. I am so incredibly grateful to you for that. Alas, I must now go for it is up to you, my boy. Nurture and protect them as they arise upon the calling of two worlds."

David then turned to Andreas and smiled softly upon him. "Thank you, Uncle, bid you farewell for now."

"Farewell my boy," Andreas responded before opening out his six massive wings and vanishing off into the either of the Celestial Realm.

Chapter 12
The Titan

Later that night, as Kenneth lay pondering silently alone in his bed, he could not begin to help himself wondering upon the recent events and that of his new calling as he lay still, staring out at the stars in the sky with the golden-red quiver firmly in hand.

He then turned his gaze away from the window and towards that of Christian Sparks' bed. But despite the sweet tranquillity of silence, Kenneth pondered curiously as to why the bubbling, blue-eyed blond was not in the bed next to his and snoring away like a loud baby elephant.

"Where is he?" Kenneth sighed as he quietly snuck up out of his bed. "Christian?" he silently whispered as he prowled down the stairs where the blue-eyed blond had peacefully dwelt.

And so, upon finding the bubbling teenage boy sitting alone within the perfectly kept living room, Kenneth gazed curiously down upon him from the bottom of the manor staircase, all the while the young boy focused in on the electrical charges that flowed within and all around him. Kenneth then commenced to study on as Christian stood mysteriously atop one of Lucy's pristine, silver house lamps as he gently waved his hands back and forth.

"Is that your crystal ball?" Kenneth chuckled suddenly.

The astounded young Christian Sparks leaped up in sheer horror and shrieked like a little girl as the electrical charge from within his hands suddenly made the bulb explode and shatter upon Lucy's aqua-green carpet.

"Kenneth what are you doing scaring me like that?" the blue-eyed blond asked as his hands began to clear of the glowing electrical discharge.

"Oops, sorry," Kenneth sniggered playfully. "We best change the bulb and clean that up before your mom wakes up."

Christian then rolled his eyes in bemusement as he swiftly and silently turned towards the kitchen like a freckled-faced ninja. "So, you had to spy on me while I practice getting used to this power," he asked.

"Christian," Kenneth sighed. "We have a calling now."

"Oh yes. A calling to clear up any mess that we make, or by god our greatest nemesis will be that of the fabled and fearsome banshee mother cry," Christian chuckled as he pulled a spare lightbulb from the kitchen drawers along with a red and glossy small brush with an equally red and glossy shovel to match.

"You know, now that I think upon it Christian," Kenneth commenced as the young, blue-eyed blond began to sweep and clean away the glassy debris. "If my uncle, Andreas, really is an Archangel, then maybe I am too. Or, at least part of me is anyway."

Christian then chuckled while he screwed the new lightbulb into that of his mother's exquisite silver house lamp. "It is as David said, Kenneth, apparently Andreas was sent to protect us before the coming of our gifts."

"Yeah but I don't feel like I actually belong amongst most people in life," Kenneth sighed calmly.

"Neither do most teenagers, Kenneth. We like to call them emos these days," Christian explained bluntly. "Now if you don't mind, I would actually like to become acquainted with my new electrokinetic abilities."

Just then, Kenneth accidently began to ignite a small flame upon that of Lucy's quiet and smouldering amber fireplace.

"Oh, crap!" Kenneth yelped as he and Christian quickly chucked a vase of water upon the newly sparked and crackling flames.

"I am telling you this, Kenneth," Christian gasped through adrenaline fuelled panic. "If my mom ever figures out about our powers, she'll definitely flip for sure... Well, probably after safe proofing the house and car, but still."

"Don't you worry about a thing, Christian!" Kenneth exclaimed under his breath as he patted the blue-eyed blond atop his back. "We'll all get used to having these abilities. David will still be around to teach us control. So, I suggest that we should all go back to see him as soon as we can."

Not too long after congregating together in the living room, the boys decided to return quietly to their beds where they remained until Lucy summoned the ranks for an early feast of breakfast delights at the breaking of another glorious dawn.

"It's ready!" the petite redhead exclaimed as the sound of cooking could be heard sizzling away in the background behind her. "Uppy, up, up, my darlings mustn't be late."

"Mm smells great," Emma sighed as she and Naomi tiredly carried theirselves into the dining area where breakfast was served mightily once more. "I could honestly get used to this."

"Thank you, Emma," Lucy smiled as she began to plate up the food. "Did either of you hear anything last night?"

Emma silently shook her head as she commenced onto eating her food.

"It was probably nothing Mom," Naomi yawned in response.

"Hmm," Lucy sighed as she began to narrow her eyeline at the two exhausted boys who were both pulling themselves into the dining room like a defeated couple of dying cats. "No matter, breakfast is ready, so let us all eat before I drive you off for another day of school."

***

11 am once more. And Kenneth, Naomi and Eric soon found themselves sitting at the front desks of none other than their poetically challenged history teacher, Mr McKenzie.

"Hmm," Kenneth pondered as he clung tightly onto his now shrunken quiver all the while Mr McKenzie rambled on to the class about the legacy of the Grecian Titans.

And so, just then, suddenly came an eruption of intense flames in the trash cans of the classroom and outer hallway as the magics channelled by Kenneth's Artefact amplified the range of the Piolan Warrior's powers.

"Not again!" Peter McKenzie yelped as he quickly lunged through the classroom doors so to shatter the fire alarm case and alert the whole school towards the immediate danger. "Everyone with me, stay in a single file and go into the parking lot where we will wait until further notice.

Kenneth however did not decide to follow along with the other students into the safety of the parking lot. And in doing so, he increased the size of his magical quiver before jumping out of the classroom window to sneak away to the sanctuary of David's hideout at Angel Falls Park. "Now that's how to use your powers…" he chuckled aloud to himself as he darted off around the trees that lead on up towards the park.

"Warrior of Fire…" a strange distorted voice then sounded. "How long I have waited."

"Who's there?" Kenneth asked as he swiftly gazed around at the woodland yard which was now quickly shrouded in the darkness of the induced fire's smoke.

Kenneth was suddenly, quickly and swiftly lifted up off of his feet and then tossed aside like a toy before crashing into one of the many large palm trees that stood guard between the school and cliff faces at Angel Falls Park.

Reacting on pure instinct, Kenneth then ignited a flame just above his left hand so that he could in fact illuminate the blacked-out path on which he stood.

"I was long told of your destined arrival…" the ominous voice echoed amongst the trees in a wave of spooky sounds. "And now that I have you here, I shall indeed use your aura to once again revive my Titan powers."

"Who the hell are you?" Kenneth exclaimed as the eerie voice continued to circle him amongst the smoked-out woodland.

But he was once again raised up from the ground by the strange, cloaked figure before being launched into the hard body of yet another large palm tree.

"It was Piolan magic which stripped me of my Godly and great powers," the voice chuckled rather sinisterly as the figure slipped amongst the shadows of the smoke and trees. "And so, it will be again that the Piolan magics which have defaced me of my powers will in fact be the very magics to restore me to my once and former glory."

"Leave him alone!" Christian exclaimed as he violently struck the darkly cloaked figure with a rather immensely striking bolt of blue and white lightning.

"And then there were two…" the voice cackled as suddenly the black smoke from the fire quickly began to dissipate along with the echoing laughter of the hooded and ominous stranger.

And so, as the boys gazed up into the clearing, they had in fact seen that the hooded stranger had all but gone and left without a single trace.

"What was that?" Christian asked as he studied Kenneth's dirty and much cindered face.

"The Greek Titan, it has to be Mr McKenzie for sure," Kenneth gasped as he shrunk away his stunning, golden-feathered quiver.

"No Kenneth," Christian responded. "Mr McKenzie is still around at the parking lot with the rest of the school teachers and students."

Kenneth gave a swift glance of confusion before noticing that he was still in fact holding a ball of fire within his left hand. "I didn't mean to make this happen," he spoke while dousing the burning ball between the palms of his hands. "I need a cool drink."

And as the boys quickly made their way back towards the parking lot, Christian waved over at the teacher whom Kenneth had suspected of attacking him merely moments before. "If it wasn't for Mr McKenzie, then I wouldn't have found you, Kenneth."

"Did you say something?" Kenneth muttered as his eyes remained fixed upon the poetically humbling and mysterious teacher of historical accuracies.

"Kenneth, hello," Christian said as he waved his hands in front of his older cousin's face. "Anybody home…?"

Chapter 13
The Dream in Tale

Once all classes had ended for the day, Kenneth had once again decided to sneak off out of the school grounds and into the wilderness of the town's national landmark, Angel Falls Park. "Here goes nothing!" the dark-haired boy muttered aloud while once again enlarging the size of his magical Piolan quiver.

***

Meanwhile, back at the school, however, Christian soon found himself roaming through the giant, white marble-stoned corridors towards the history classroom when something rather odd caught hold of his attention, coming from inside of the rather small janitor's broom cupboard.

"Oh my god, what are you two doing in here?" the blue-eyed blond gasped as he coincidently walked in on Claire Stevenson and Max Weatherfield snuggled together within the confines of the cosy and tight small space.

"I can explain," Claire gasped as she held onto a topless Max. "We were just. Um, we were just hiding from the fire."

"The fire...?" Christian chuckled as he rolled his big, blue eyes in disbelief. "And I'm guessing that you had to take off Max's shirt just to keep him cool of course?"

"Busted," Max sighed before slipping back on his purple, silken shirt. "What is it Christian?"

"Well, as it just so happens, Kenneth found himself under attack by a strange and ominous, hooded figure," Christian grinned as his friends quickly stepped out from within the tiny cupboard. "And it happened here on the school grounds just beyond the Angel Falls cliffs.

"Ooh, another one of those scary nun people?" Claire asked with gleaming enticement in her eyes.

"Eh, we should probably get our Artefacts and return to Angel Falls," Christian spoke. "Our powers actually increased in strength during that tussle outside."

"Wait what?" Max asked. "No offence, Christian, but I keep making things shatter whenever I get too nervous. I don't want to accidentally break anyone."

"Yeah, that's exactly why we need to figure out the way to conduct our control," Christian muttered as Claire slipped on her dazzling Piolan necklace.

"Stunning isn't it?" she chuckled playfully. "So, when do we leave?"

***

Meanwhile, as Kenneth then reached the silence of the Angelic Oasis burial grounds, he soon found himself unable to proceed forward due to the nerves of confronting this new and real threat of facing the inner demons which haunt him each and every single night.

"Okay, Kenneth, you can do this," he sighed aloud to himself before commencing forth into the light of the Celestial pocket realm.

***

Back at the school, as Christian gathered up his team of friends, he spotted Mr McKenzie cleaning up a small flesh wound which had appeared to resemble that of a striking bolt of lightning, or probably just another bee sting. "Kenneth's overthinking is really beginning to give me a headache," the blue-eyed blond sighed as he proceeded away from the classroom to meet the others at the front of the school yard.

***

All the while back at Angel Falls, Kenneth had finally reached the large mansion which housed the grandeur Guardian-angel David himself. "My dream, my eye, do you know anything?" he sighed as suddenly…

Kenneth instantly found himself standing within the luxurious and lavish lounge room after chapping on the great and grand doors merely moment before.

"Well done," David smiled. "You're figuring out the use of your powers. And, of course, you can only enter into my domain with your Artefact in hand. Although, I'm guessing you probably figured that one out already?"

"My dream, you see. I've been seeing it for as long as I can remember. I'm six years old at the time, and there is a violent thunderstorm crashing overhead atop a mysterious mountain," Kenneth suddenly began to say.

David, however, just gazed at him through his mysteriously big, moonlit blue eyes, "Go on."

"A lady, a beautiful redheaded woman, also stands atop this mountain. And I am not standing that far behind her as many blurry figures all clamour to escape. And she has this intense red necklace amulet thingy with her," he continues. "I scream at her, but everything becomes indistinct as a clap of thunder blurs out the sounds in my mind! And then I crash into her, and the necklace shatters in my face, right into my left eye!" he continued while pointing out his ruby-red eyes.

But, David just commenced to gaze on at him in complete hypnotic silence.

"I scream. Every night I scream to myself. And I'm there, I can feel it, David, it haunts me every single night," Kenneth spoke through a husky and broken tone. "I don't know why or if it's got something to do with your name but I feel safe talking to you. Just like I felt when Uncle Andreas was still around."

"I see," David sighed as he folded over his majestic and muscular arms. "You will get to see your uncle again one day, Kenneth. And as for your father, I am truly sorry."

"Is the woman in my dream an Oracle? The one from the stories that my uncle used to tell me about, the one that had to leave because she was forever changed for facing off against the darkness?" the young teen asked cautiously.

"No," David responded softly as he continued to gaze curiously upon the troubled teen. "Black no longer resides among the people of this world."

"Who is she?" Kenneth sobbed softly. "If it isn't this Black, then who is she?"

Looking up and making steady eye contact with Kenneth, David softly placed both hands atop the Warrior's shoulders as he began to explain, "Two brothers, two entities cut from the same cloth. The All and The Nothing. This woman that you speak of from your dreams is in fact the Celestial Goddess of the cosmos. Her name is Red."

"Why would she haunt me so?" he continued to weep softly.

David gently placed his hand atop the aggrieved teenager's back as he softly commenced forth to speak, "I cannot say. Nor is it my place to explain such things. But the dream that you have been repeating will eventually come to a close. You are not ready yet, my boy. Not for this."

"Oh, yeah, I was also jumped on my way over here," Kenneth sighed while wiping clean his misty, red eyes. "He was a crazy, strong, ominous, hooded figure that called himself a Titan."

David gazed away from the teenager as his expression became solid, "Prometheus," the Celestial suddenly exclaimed. "He has found you. And now that he knows that you are all here, he will next be searching for the Dagger of the Circle, the Celestial blade from the Archangel of Earth. The King Autt himself."

"Wait what?" Kenneth sighed as he then passed the Celestial a sudden confounded expression.

"There's no time to lose Kenneth," David expressed vigorously. "As from this moment onward, I shall begin training you all. For it is now the time that you and the others become the famed and greatly destined anticipated Warriors of Piathos."

Chapter 14
Falling into the Summer End

Friday, October 24, 2008. Angelic Oasis.

Several weeks had since passed before the breeze of fall had begun to shed and sweep the Oasis from the vast waves and winds of the sea. And the now newly-formed Warriors of Piathos were however, coming into their powers and skills quite nicely.

"Costumes, oh how I just love dressing up for Halloween, oh and happy birthday, Naomi," Sarah squealed as she handed Naomi a card which was concealed within a very pink and bright, bubbly envelope.

"Hmm," Naomi sighed with a smile as she accepted the birthday card which Sarah had written especially for her. "What a coincidence that I get a gift card within my birthday card as we shop together at the great Angels Mall."

"You like it?" Sarah smirked as the girls continued along through the shopping centre.

"Of course, I do," Naomi smiled before cuddling into her blonde-headed friend.

"Now, Naomi you pick first," Claire chuckled as the girls entered into the 'small mall costume shop'. "What do you want to be for Halloween?"

"Hmm," the dark-haired girl sighed, "Something that has actually sacred me, I know. I'll be a nun."

Claire gazed wondrously upon Naomi with a bewildered expression before turning her head to ask, "A nun? Hmm, ooh very scary indeed. I call dibs, so Naomi you should be a witch."

"A witch," Naomi chuckled as both Sarah and Emma suddenly scampered around the shop with costumes of glittery cuteness.

On the other side of the store, however, the boys were all throwing toys at each other while picking out their own costumes for the upcoming Halloween festivities. "I'm a pirate!" Kenneth shouted as he and Christian both jumped around inside of the isle like a pair of excitable kittens.

Paul, on the other hand, searched quietly throughout the costume display until he happened upon a rather charmingly lavish and green navy costume. "Oh, I do like this," he chuckled, all the while Max and Josh crossed toy swords very loudly in the farther background of the store's isle.

***

Later on, however as the day passed on and of course after Lucy had filled the teens up on dinner and birthday cake, the team had decided to take their Artefacts and go back to the park so that they could return to the majesty of David's Celestial pocket ream.

"Hey, do you guys know anything about the abandoned manor which has been locked off at the far end of the island?" Eric asked as the team strolled along by the lakes and streams that flowed rather quaintly from the large and majestic waterfall.

"The abandoned manor house, can't say that I've even ever heard of it?" Kenneth spoke as the golden rays of dusk danced elegantly upon the waters reflection as they walked on by.

"What about it?" Naomi interrupted as Kenneth suddenly zoned into the town's tale with intrigue and interest.

"Well, it's quite an interesting tale actually," Eric began. "In the mid to late 18th century, there lived a rich and noble family at the very edge of the town on this very island. And their home was said to sit atop a portal that lead into an underworld dimension of mystical properties."

"We should all go and visit this place on Halloween night," Claire chuckled as she lunged in on the story from behind the boys.

"It was also stated that a good and powerful witch soon placed an enchantment atop the house after a great tragedy struck at the heart of their home," Eric continued as the teens soon passed on through the walk at the base of the giant waterfall.

"Is it really wise to go out there though?" Paul chuckled nervously in response to Claire's question. "Especially when there are crazy nuns and hooded villains out there, we shouldn't test fate just because we haven't seen anything since June."

"There were rumours of a dark being that tried to enter but many times did he fail because of the good witch that resided nearby," Eric continued. "Up until in the late 1800s, there was an assassination of the entire family, and only one of them had survived the monstrosity of the massacre… Violet Rose," Eric's voice enticed Kenneth, as he spoke.

"Oh, so how does it make the house haunted?" Kenneth asked as the team tarried on while Eric vigorously commenced on with the tragic tale.

"Going mad with grief, Violet then called out to the witch who had sheltered the portal with a spell and asked for her help in destroying the monster responsible for killing her entire family. But when the good witch refused her hand in killing, poor Violet was left with nothing but her empty home. And so, cried out. She screamed that no one would ever breach the walls of her forsaken home again," the figure skater exclaimed passionately.

"You sound just like good old Peter McKenzie," Naomi sarcastically chuckled in response.

"And then what happened?" Kenneth pondered deeply as curiosity continued to flow within his eyes.

"She took her own life, of course. Just before begging anyone who could hear her that the house should become cursed upon her untimely demise so that no one may enter, and so I digress," Eric continued. "The beings that resided among the underworld realm had decreed it in their best interest. And of course, they granted her wish. But instead of offering her peace and justice, she was ultimately left alone to guard the house from unwanted intruders for all time."

"Whoa… How weird is that? Do you think it could have been the Titan who tried to gain entry into the underworld portal?" Kenneth asked eagerly.

Just then however, a dark and ominous figure swiftly scurried on by the team as it knocked them over like a row of skittles in one sweep.

"Not again!" Kenneth grunted as he swiftly jumped up and ignited a fire in both of his hands. "I know who you are!" he exclaimed as the other Warriors quickly summoned their Artefacts into their larger sizes.

"Come and see… You may be surprised," the distorted voice eerily taunted from the growing shadows of the autumn nightfall.

"You bet ya!" Kenneth answered as he ran off into the further layouts of the Oasis cemetery.

"Kenneth, wait!" Emma called out as the team quickly followed behind.

Just then, a bolt of lightning shot past Kenneth and knocked the Titan further into the darkness as the villain quickly attempted to grab hold of his cousin and run.

And upon arriving at the corner of the great and large marble mausoleums however, the Warriors of Piathos were met with a massively hulking figure which dressed in what appeared to be that of shining, shimmering black armour.

And along with the pristine, Grecian type armour that he wore below his cloak, the heavy and giant male figure also wore that of an unworldly full helmet which appeared almost as awe-striking as it did horrific. The entire coat of the ethereal armour which was only slightly similar to David's seemed to reflect that of a far off and distant image. However, instead of showing the glowing gleams of a stunning blue sky, the armour which was worn by the seven-feet-tall assailant reflected that of the imagery to each gazer worst and most frighteningly dreaded memories.

"I told you," the ominous voice spoke robustly. "Piolan magic will be the return of my great and godly powers…"

And so just then, the ten Warriors of Piathos were suddenly met with the horrific images of their most dreaded and worst-lived, memorable experiences.

"Try as you might, but I am draped in the darkest of Mystical Artefacts," the Titan laughed mockingly as he reached out to grab hold of Kenneth again.

"Wait," Sarah sighed as suddenly the clear jewels that sat elegantly within her tiara began to glow in bright bursts of gleaming pink energy. "It's an enchantment!" she called out as through her eyes the tiara had instantly opened her mind to the illusions. "Guys, wake up!"

Gazing around for a moment, Sarah spotted three loose boulders sitting atop the fertile grass merely a few foot-steps from where they were standing.

And just before the Titan could strike at the petrified Warriors, Sarah had then grabbed hold of the rocks with her mind's eye before violently, telekinetically launching the boulders at the armoured assailant.

Taking a hard blast from the rocky attack, the Titan then turned his attention towards that of the blue-eyed blonde girl as she faced him off with her stunning and gleaming tiara.

"Warrior of the Mind..." he grunted while slowly making chase for her. "I may have lost my powers, but you are all still no real match for me."

Just then, however, as he stalked horrifyingly towards the girl in the dark of the graveyard, the Titan soon found himself being bound to the Earth by that of Paul's coiling and entwining roots.

"You stay the hell away from my sister..." Paul muttered as he and the others soon fought their way through the petrification of the enchanted terror. "Sarah, go and summon David," he groaned though the strains.

"You may have your little Guardian-Angel at hand," the Titan spoke as he easily tore through the roots as if they were made of mushy paper. "But once I receive the Artefact which remains hidden deep within the haunted Hell House, I shall then slay him with his own kin's blade and make you watch as he is taken from your very grasp."

And so just then, Joshua Stevenson swiftly landed the armoured Titan a mean backhander. And with his intensely mighty super-strength, he suddenly knocked the villain right through the walls of the old stone mausoleum.

"Let's get back to the gateway," Eric muttered while summoning to the ground a billowing wave of thick white mist. "This should keep him down for a while."

"Neat trick," Claire squealed as she grabbed hold of Eric's Hawaii shirt and pulled him back towards the gate meanwhile the fog quickly shrouded the burial grounds. "Now come on."

Not more than ten minutes had passed before the Warriors of Piathos were safely hidden within the confines of the Celestial pocket realm.

"It intrigues me that he has only attacked you twice now in the past few months," David spoke curiously through a pondering tone. "It appears to me that he actually wants to induce the growth of your individual powers."

"Yeah but why, what's his motive?" Emma asked as Billy swept through the lounge room with a silver tray of hot blueberry muffins.

"Believe me. This also mystifies even my wondrous mind…" David answered as he continued to ponder deeply. "The most logical answer is that he needs you to retrieve something for him. Something, something cursed. Yes, something that even he cannot gain access to."

"The Hell House," Kenneth exclaimed as he snapped his fingers together. "The story that you were telling me about, Eric, there has to be something really special hidden in there. The Dagger of the Circle, it must be hidden there?"

"Rose Manor," Eric sighed. "Even if the blade is out there, who's not to say that we aren't just playing into the Titan's hands?"

Kenneth then turned his head eagerly towards David as realisation suddenly struck like a spark, "The underworld realm, that's where the Titan is trying to go, and the Dagger of Autt must be the only way through for him."

David then passed the young Warrior a slight grin, showing that he in fact knew what the frantic teenager was actually ranting on about. "That place is a mystical hotspot for all of those who do possess the means in bartering change for their past, present and future."

"You sure do seem to know a lot about this place," Naomi chuckled as she folded over her arms and sighed. "So, what is really down there, David?"

Passing the dark-haired girl a rather coy glance, David in drew a deep breath and nodded his head as he began to speak, "The Circle of Destiny… You see that house shelters the only way in and out of the fiery domain which safeguards all of the

Earth's fallen deities. And it seems that Prometheus is out to regain the ways which his kin once coveted."

Naomi suddenly dropped her guard as she in turn kindly retuned the nod of good gesture to that of the Celestial Being.

"Tread carefully Warriors. If I could accompany you in man's world on the outside then it would make all of this a whole lot easier," David spoke firmly. "But ever since The Great Betrayal, we are now forbidden to intervene in the affairs of mankind. But I digress you must work together as one single unit. Prometheus is as wise as he is cunning and if he should retrieve his divine godly powers and journey to The Circle of Destiny, then there is no telling what the council would offer him in return for that Celestial Artefact..."

Chapter 15
Halloween Festivities

Friday, October 31, All Hallows' Eve, Angelic Oasis.

"We must have everything ready precisely for tonight's grand festivities at the marvellous home of Joseph Weatherfield himself," Lucy exclaimed excitedly whilst she danced around the dining area dressed in the most overwhelming fairy godmother garments of sparkling and glittering blue.

"Sure you've got enough food there to take with you Mom?" Naomi asked as she entered into the dining room dressed as a fierce and silver-armoured Valkyrie.

"Does a mother ever have too much, my darling?" Lucy chuckled as the front doorbell suddenly began to chime. "Now then Naomi, be a dear and answer the front door, would you? Oh, and cover up your legs sweetie. It's supposed be getting cold later."

"Oh, I like the cold," the Warrior of Ice chuckled in response while moving towards the Sparks Manor front door which was crowded by far too many Halloween décor placed there by Lucy herself.

And so, upon opening the front door, Naomi was met with a very happy and handsome, brunet young solider.

"Stephen," she gasped with sudden surprise. "You're back, how long have you been back?"

Stephen Lee Craig was a very tall young man of 18 who stood approximately at six-feet-seven. He was, in fact, one of the Sparks' closest friends and had decided to join the army when his parents retired to live out their golden years in the north end of the Angelic Oasis.

Stephen also had the most robust and bulky muscular form. But he equally had one of the cutest faces in contrast to his great size which Lucy had always referred to as the cheeks of a giant teddy bear. His clean-shaven appearance made him seem all that much younger. As did his bright green emerald eyes which glistened in the rays of the late evening autumn sun.

"Stephen dear, so good to see you," Lucy sang as she swiftly pranced towards him like the fairy godmother that she truly was. "Come in my dear boy, please won't you give a hand?"

The tall, green-eyed soldier then gave a smirk as Emma Feather swiftly and elegantly glided down the stairs dressed as the most charming and beautiful mermaid. She was however quickly followed behind by Christian Sparks who dawned that of the armour of a valiant and handsome white knight.

Upon spotting each other however, Stephen and Christian instantly passed between them the largest of grins before commencing forth into embracing one another.

"Stephen, I'm so glad to see that you're back," the blue-eyed blond exclaimed with excitement. "How long are you here for?"

"Just until next week," the tall, dark and handsome man responded, all the while Kenneth soon descended the stairs dressed in the black and red garments of a true and noble Japanese Samurai.

"Stephen," Lucy called out as she swiftly returned to the food-packed dining room. "I'd like you to meet my niece and nephew, Kenneth and Emma Feather."

"Pleased to meet your acquaintance," he smiled kindly while shaking the siblings' hands in a humbled and quaint greeting. "It's really good to meet you guys."

Just then, however, Lucy suddenly began to trot back into the living room with trays of sealed food towering in her hands, "Children time to leave. The party is waiting… And so is my Martini!"

"Here. Let me assist you to my car with these trays," Stephen said as he and Christian quickly loaded the twelve plates of sandwiches, casseroles, pizzas, puddings and cakes into the trunk of Stephen Craig's giant and impressive, camouflaged, navy Land Rover.

***

No more than an hour had passed before Lucy and Stephen had soon arrived at the giant and quaint mansion of Weatherfield Corporations where a few of the other Warriors waited patiently for the family to arrive.

"Whoa," Kenneth gasped in awe as he gazed on up at the humungous house which seemed to be stretched over eighty acres of land with rivers that lead into a fort and forest which surrounded the estate in overwhelming majesty and glory.

"Oh my god, Claire, what have you done?" Naomi gasped as they met the others in the parking lot just inside of the circular fort. "You weren't kidding when you said you were going to be a nun... But come on?"

"Oh, I'm not just a nun, Naomi. I'm a bad nun!" Claire chuckled as she proceeded to open up the front of her habit to reveal her cleavage which was embraced within her tight-laced, black corset. "Titty power..."

"She looks absolutely amazing," Max sighed as he hugged tightly on to his air-bending lover. "It would be a sin not to admire such wholesome beauty," the young Warrior chuckled as he stood before the team dressed in the most expensive of golden Egyptian armoury.

"Rescue me from this madness," Josh sighed as he stepped forward dressed in the most traditional of vampire garments. "My cousin has been showing off all day and Max here has been completely idle to say the least."

"Hey, when a woman wants to feel empowered," Max chuckled as Sarah and Paul soon arrived just behind the Sparks family.

"Whoa, Sarah you look incredible," Kenneth sighed upon the radiant beauty which she was. "What perfection do you appear as before me?"

Sarah stood sturdily yet elegantly before the group with her long blonde hair flowing out in wisps and waves as the evening breeze passed by. And so, on her body she wore that of the most delicate, purest and softest, billowing, pink silk.

"I be Aphrodite," she smiled in kind, "the Greek deity of love..."

"And I be Dionysus," Paul spoke as he stood before the group dressed in the finest of white satin which was laced with green vines, leaves and pink, blooming blossom flowers. "The Greek deity of fertility, fine wine and an all-round good time…"

"Damn," Stephen gasped as he and Lucy had just finished carting the many trays into the large and pristine Weatherfield estate. "You Blossomes surely never fail to blossom, I mean whoa, you guys look amazing."

"Stephen," Paul grinned excitedly at the sight of his great and beloved childhood friend, "you made it back."

Christian then turned his blushing gaze towards that of Stephen Craig as he stood graciously and mighty before the bustling ballroom party. The tall and handsome soldier, however, caught sight of the blue-eyed blond who returned his admiration with a smile in kind.

And so, upon arriving into the huge mansion of their comrade and great friend, Maximus Weatherfield, Kenneth and the other Warriors were then guided into the large and majestic great hall which bustled with that of live music, ballroom dancing and other traditional festivities.

"Children, this is the home of the Weatherfield Corporations leader, owner and founder, the great entrepreneur himself, Joseph Weatherfield," Lucy smirked as she glided quaintly into the busy and bustling ballroom.

Not too far behind everyone else, soon arrived Eric Tony who was accompanied by both of his adoring and wonderful parents. The young Japanese American then ascended down into the great hall dressed in the exact same ninja armour as Kenneth Feather himself.

"Whoa, it suits him way more than it suits me," Kenneth exclaimed wide-eyed in surprise as he tarried beside the fruit punch-bowl accompanied by the beautiful Emma Feather and Sarah Blossome.

***

And as the hands of the Weatherfield's grandfather's clock passed on into the late hours of the night, the Warriors of Piathos had then quickly rallied together by the grand staircase with their Artefacts firmly in hand.

"Rose Manor resides on the abandoned road which is just outside of the estate," Max spoke while fitting on his duel silver gauntlets. "This really doesn't go with my costume, does it?" he pondered while gazing down at the Artefacts which glistened brightly on his hands.

Just then, however, Lucy could be heard singing in the background in a rather abrupt and overwhelming fashion as she danced the night away. All the while she was being dwarfed in size as she boogied like mad with the tall and charming Stephen.

"Are you sure that we'll be back in time before everyone notices that we've actually all gone?" Emma asked as she clutched tightly onto her glowing-blue trident.

Christian then gazed up at his mother all the while she danced merrily in hand with the many people from her beloved job and said, "Don't worry, I told her that we were all going for a stroll around the gardens of the estate."

"Okay. That's 10.15," Kenneth muttered while strapping the golden and red quiver firmly onto his back. "We've been here for four hours now. And so, it's now time that we all move swiftly into action. Prometheus may not be too far, and I haven't sighted Peter at this party yet."

"Come on," Naomi exclaimed as the frost on her sword glistened brightly like freshly fallen snow that lay atop an icy lake. "It's time that we had some real fun."

Chapter 16
The Hell House

No more than twenty minutes had passed before the ten young Warriors of Piathos had left the pristine gardens of Weatherfield Corporations and stepped foot out onto the old abandoned and eerie road of the condemned and infertile wastelands.

"Liberate thee from thine curse…"

A haunting voice whispered in the passing cold gusts as the teenagers soon crept upon the infamous and uncanny, tall, black house which stood comfortably in ruin amongst its dank surroundings.

"Though hath come to set thee free…"

The sounds of ghostly wailing quickly echoed around the building which stood in the decay of the vast, dark woodlands and ominously spooky crevasses.

"Claire, that gust was you, right?" Josh asked as he and the others gazed fearfully upon the great house which shuddered ominously in the wind. The manor was also completely coated in damp moss and was also being bound by that of a brisk and wiry overgrowth.

"Um, no," the sexy nun shivered while closing over her unbuttoned nunnery habit. "But hey. If she can talk through the wind, then so can I."

"Wait, what?" Josh squealed as his cousin drew in a deep breath of cold and damp air.

And so, upon releasing a sharp and cold breeze back at the eerie old house, Claire slowly began to exclaim her vocal tone through a mighty gust of strong and howling winds.

"WHOOOOOO AREEEE YOUUUUU?" she sang through the sinister howl of the houses groans. "AAAAAAAAARRREE YOUUUUU ROOOOOOOOOOOOOSEEEE? I AM CLAIRE. PLEASE LET US IN, AAAH AHH AHHH AHH AAAHHH... TITTYY POOOOOWWWWEEERRR..."

"Is she seriously singing?" Emma aggressively called out.

But suddenly, the strong gales that were being drawn down from the dark skies by Claire were then quickly ceased. And the ungodly cries which had ominously resonated from within the cold and unforgiving, forsaken Hell House, swiftly replied with another creepy whisper.

"Only thou sublime one..."

And so just then, Kenneth was suddenly yanked up from his ankles by something that could only be described as an insanely powerful magnet haul as he was dragged across the dead infertile yard and pulled into the cold and unforgiving shadowy home.

"Kenneth!" Emma screamed as suddenly she created a body of water from the moisture of the atmosphere which was cold and damp all around her. "Let him go!" she cried as she swung her arm at the wave causing it to crash into the shuddering door as it once again sealed itself shut.

"This is scary and on Halloween of all nights!" Sarah cried as she quickly lunged herself into that of Emma Feather's arms.

"Ssh, don't worry. My brother will fight this," Emma answered nervously. "We just have to figure out a way to get into that house."

***

Upon opening his eyes after the pulling and dragging had all but halted, Kenneth could clearly see that of what appeared to be an odd projection of a noble woman that had a head of dark hair which was tied up to perfection in a spirally style of the 18th century. He could also see that she dawned that of a violet and silken frock which glided along with her as she suddenly fazed into and out of existence.

"Are you real?" Kenneth asked while he swiftly jumped back up onto his feet. "Violet Rose?"

The obscure young female whose appearance was transparent and glassy seemed to also flicker like a light around him as she spoke. "How lonely thou hath been," she whispered coldly. "But it is thy price in exchange for sanctuary of thy home."

Kenneth however lit a ball of fire that he held just atop his left hand so that he could in fact illuminate the environment which stayed frozen in a capsule of time all around him. And so, upon glancing around at the dimly lit room, he could see that he was in fact standing within a chamber which housed the bones of the fair maiden's body.

"Can my friends come in?" he asked cautiously.

"Nae," she answered sharply while flickering ominously in and out of Kenneth's sight. "Thy curse doth not grant passage to thou whom may walk. Only thou whom art sublime may enter…"

Kenneth then studied Violet as she suddenly began to glitch down a dark and winding hallway.

"Cometh sublime one," her voice carried coldly. "We hath not much time before thou monster returns."

***

Meanwhile on the outside, Naomi and the others were swiftly continuing to search the house for any and all available entrances to the inside of the dark and dank home. "It's like the house can't actually be breached," the icy Warrior then grunted and groaned in sheer frustration. "The windows keep getting too high, and the doors keep going out of whack. Honestly, I feel like I'm going dizzy out of my mind."

Just then, however, Sarah's tiara once again began to glow as it sat quaintly atop her head. And so, her powers of the mind suddenly began to stir like a vortex deep inside as she began to wish herself to be by Kenneth's side… And so, just then, Sarah quickly vanished into the pink gleam of her Divine Artefact which set off a sudden shockwave of energy from around where she stood. And as a result, the space where she stood instantly became stunned by the lack of matter and then ruptured violently as it quickly began to repair itself.

"Did my sister just explode?" Paul yelped from the sudden surprise.

"In here!" Sarah's voice could be heard clearly coming from the inside of the walls of haunted Hell House. "The house is a trick of some kind," she called out from within the dank and cold lounge room all the while studying its appearance for a way to open an entrance. "Let me help you inside."

"Josh, over here," Paul exclaimed as the group quickly began to follow the clear and sharp sounds of Sarah's sweet voice. "Punch it open."

***

Elsewhere at the base of the house, Kenneth swiftly followed on behind the flickering and glassy image as the ghost of Violet Rose until suddenly she came to a halt inside of a room which ignited in the flames of a Celestial torch upon Kenneth Feather's arrival. The Warrior of Fire then gazed longingly up at the pristine and golden torch as it sat idly atop an ancient stone sarcophagus.

"Whoa, what is that?" the surprised Warrior sighed as he doused the burning flame which he held vigorously atop his left hand.

"Taketh thine Artefact sublime one," she whispered hauntingly into his ears all the while remaining stationed just before the burning torch. "Taketh thine Artefact and liberate thee from thine curse."

"I'll liberate you bitch!" Naomi's voice sounded harshly in the background as the nine other Warriors quickly came charging into the ominous and chilling altar room.

"UNWELCOME…!" Violet's voice cried out in a bloodcurdling scream.

"Too right unwelcome," the Warrior of Ice chuckled cockily in response.

"Wait, Naomi, wait!" Kenneth called out as he swiftly made pace towards the cone torch which sat firmly atop the old and dusty sarcophagus.

And just as Kenneth pulled the blazing torch from its stand, the entire manor suddenly began to tremble and shake as the curse which kept outsiders from entering suddenly began to break away.

Just then, after the tremendous quake had all but ceased, suddenly came peace and solace to the tortured soul's eyes. Violet Rose stood still, gazing onward at Kenneth as she once again began to fade away.

"Only thou sublime could lift thine Artefact," she muttered while commencing to give a genuine smile. "Over three hundred years, I hath guarded thy home. But thy home was doomed to protect ye realm which exists on thy portal below thy floor…"

And so just then, Violet Rose all but ceased to exist as she once and for all faded from sight.

Chapter 17
Blazing Torch

Not too long after exiting the creepy, old Hell House did the Warriors of Piathos once again found themselves standing face-to-face with the black-armoured Titan, Prometheus, on the dark and winding road mere minutes away from the Weatherfield estate.

"Well done," the armoured assailant chuckled as he pulled from his back a long and sturdy glowing purple chain. "No more games, no more exercises. Your powers will be the return of mine."

"I don't think so," Eric yelled as he raised his arms to summon another wave of paralysing fog.

But suddenly, Eric soon found himself being bound by the chains which then tuned bright red upon contact of his skin. And without a moment to react, Prometheus then moved at a blurry super speed to push the other Warriors firmly from their stances.

"I can't use my powers!" the Warrior of Mist cried before being hauled in by the tall and deadly Titan.

"Get your hands off of him!" Josh roared as he attempted to super-punch the enemy aside. But, nonetheless he also found himself being bound and dragged in by the seven-foot-tall monster.

"My powers, they are gone!" Josh cried as Prometheus next made a move for the others.

Thinking on pure instinct, Kenneth then swung the torch like a baseball bat and upon making contact with the Titan, the torch ignited as it hurtled the assailant aside with great force.

"That is one of Autt's lanterns," Prometheus gasped. "No matter, I'll be right back..." And from his back, he whirled around himself a crimson red cape which carried him off with Eric Tony and Josh Stevenson in hand.

"My cousin, he just took my cousin!" Claire exclaimed as the Titan vanished into a vortex of pure red energy.

"I thought he didn't have his powers back yet, how is he doing all of this?" Max yelled as the other Warriors stood together from the attack.

"Come on, it isn't over yet," Kenneth said. "You guys go back to the estate, and I'll double back to Angel Falls Park."

"Kenneth, it's almost midnight," Emma gasped as she studied the blue watch that sat nicely upon her right arm.

"He won't kill them," Kenneth exclaimed. "He said this torch belongs to the Archangel Autt. So, I bet this is what Prometheus is really looking for."

"What are we supposed to tell everyone?" Paul asked through anxious woe. "We were all together when this happened... We could get done for suspected murder?"

Sarah then slapped her big brother on the back of his head and said, "Don't panic. Prometheus was really quick there, and we have to think of how we're going to rescue the boys from his grasp?"

"Sarah," Naomi gasped with the spark of sudden realisation. "You do realise that you actually teleported to find Kenneth, right?"

"She did?" Kenneth blushed.

"Shut up," Naomi interrupted. "What I mean is can't you do it again just to find where good old Titan has taken the boys too?"

"I honestly don't know." she responded softly.

"We're all done for!" Paul began to sob again.

"Dude, seriously stop overthinking," Max muttered as he tried rather hard himself to think. "I need to overthink..."

"Honey that big bad man just stole Eric and my cousin," Claire muttered to her pondering and wondering boyfriend. "How am I supposed to go home and explain to my dad and Uncle John that an actual myth magically appeared and whisked off with my cousin in hand?"

"Kenneth," Emma spoke through trembling woe, "I just want to go home."

"It's going to be okay," he reassured her calmly. "We..." Kenneth then halted at the sight of their enemy returning to them through the red vortex which twirled chaotically in the sky. "Scratch that, let's run!"

"Give me that Artefact!" Prometheus exclaimed as he suddenly towered atop the Warriors from the darkness of the barren wastelands.

Christian quickly reacted with a sudden bolt of striking lightning which knocked the Titan over by merely just a few feet. "Max, shatter him?" the blue-eyed blond yelped as he quickly took off with the rest of the scampering teenagers.

And as Max swiftly ran off with the group, he too swatted back his hands to cause a disruptive explosion in order to distract the black-armoured assailant.

Chapter 18
Into the Dungeon

4 pm the following day, and news of the missing boys was beginning to spread fast as fear and panic commenced to infest the Angelic Oasis like a dismal shadowy overcast.

"Good evening Lucy," Stephen spoke softly as he stood just outside of Sparks Manor dressed in the finest of his military garb.

"God, Stephen dear have you found them?" Lucy asked as she welcomed the sweet boy into her home.

"We've searched all over the Oasis and we're still looking, of course," Stephen replied as he gazed down upon Lucy who appeared to look almost sick with worry. "I have my people keeping an eye open for anything unusual and of course the police are looking thoroughly into their mysterious disappearances."

"Confound it Stephen Lee Craig!" Lucy exclaimed sharply from the foyer of her pristine and quaint darling home. "My dear, it is not you that I am having issues with. It's the law and the system," she continued to rant. "I fear for my kids as well, as they were all out there when this disaster occurred. God forbid anything ever happened to them or you, my heart couldn't cope. Please do all that you can, I am counting on you…"

"I'll do what I can," Stephen sighed in response before turning to re-join the search party outside.

"Stephen dear," Lucy muttered softly as she grabbed hold of his right arm.

"Yes ma'am?" he said as a faint smile crossed his face.

"Eight o'clock. Dinner tonight, the kids would love to have your company," Lucy spoke as she passed him a vague smile in return.

Stephen nodded his head in agreement before commencing away into the late afternoon sun outside.

"Who's that, Mom?" Naomi asked as she swiftly jogged down the stairs and into the hallway where her mother stood idly. "Mom, you okay? Looks like you've seen a ghost... I sure as hell did."

"Hmm, yes a ghost. Well it was Halloween, there are lots of ghosts to be found," Lucy answered wryly while studying up on Naomi's long, dark hair which she wore in a high-tied ponytail.

"Mom, what are you looking at?" the Warrior of Ice inquired.

"Oh, it's nothing darling. Time to prepare dinner as we have a very special guest arriving later, and I would also like to discuss college with you," Lucy muttered as she made pace towards the kitchen. "I want you to think very hard about what career path you wish to pursue, my dear, now that you have graduated from school."

Naomi shook her head in bewilderment as Emma scurried quickly into the foyer from the stairs behind her. "Is your mom still snapping? Christian is technically in hiding from the dreaded Crazy Poppins," the green-eyed redhead quietly chuckled.

Naomi folded over her arms as she crash-landed onto the aqua-blue sofa that resided within Lucy's beautifully and perfectly kept living room. "We've got to find this Titan and get the boys back. This seems just way too much for us. We're definitely out of our league."

"We can do this Naomi," Emma sighed gently as she sat down on the sofa beside her. "Okay, we can do this together. As a single unit, all we have to do is up our game."

Naomi turned her pondering gaze towards Emma as a faint expression of curiosity suddenly flittered on within her mind, "Yeah, but we are going to need all the help that we can get."

***

All the while, elsewhere, Josh soon found himself waking up inside that of a giant and rusted old cell meanwhile being tied up by what appeared to be purple glowing enchanted chains. "What's the point in having superhuman strength if I can't even snap a lousy chain?" he groaned as Eric sat silently beside him.

"No use, these Artefacts seem to dampen our abilities," Eric sighed as he continued to gaze on at the wall beyond the bars.

"Oh, come on brainpan, you're the smarts here. Help me!" Josh exclaimed loudly as he struggled through the jingling, glowing purple chains. "You know what. This is tedious. I haven't the time for this. Eric, come on get motivated. Use your smartness and get us out of here."

"What's the point, Josh?" Eric sighed tiredly in response. "We're technically just a bunch of kids that have flashy tricks up our sleeves. And our opponent is something far more spectacular. You know that in Ancient Greece, Prometheus was known as the bringer of fire. And he was also famed as the Titan of wisdom. So, no matter how intelligent his foe is, he will always be one step ahead."

"Some Warrior you are, sitting there all silent and helpless because your enemy has smart ass ways of thinking," Josh grunted in anger. "At least if Claire was here, she'd have some super dumb plan that would honestly, probably, most likely get us out of here."

A few minutes later, Max too had soon been tossed into the dingy cell with the chains tightly bound and a cut atop his forehead.

"Ouch! My head..." Max quivered from the sudden pain. "That smart ass grabbed me this morning when I attempted to go and see Claire."

Josh then lunged forward to cradle his wounded friend as he bled out on the ground before them. "Max, dude, buddy, are you okay? Your head, it's bleeding. Here, let me help you," he continued while removing his silken black vampire cape and pressed it tightly atop of Max' open wound.

"Just let it go, please," Eric grunted while curling up into a ball in the corner.

"No!" Josh shouted in anger again. "Max is injured. And if it hasn't escaped your attention, we are all locked up together inside of a dungeon. And you know what man, if that's going to be your attitude, then why do you even bother performing at the figure skating contests if you're too busy crying about your opponent's strength."

Max slowly leaned against the cold stone wall beside Josh and sighed as he swiftly commenced to speak, "Don't you worry,

156

my boy. The others will figure out a way to break us out. Especially our Claire, that girl has some nut of crazy."

Josh then laughed in response as he too sat up against the cold stone wall beside Max and said, "Yeah, let's wait for our crazy ass nun to arrive and rescue us, titty power and all."

Both boys then became silent after their laugh and watched Eric as he fell asleep in defeat just a few paces beside them. "Don't worry buddy, we'll get you out of here," Josh sighed to Eric as he closed his eyes and wept silently for his parents.

***

7:45 pm and the Sparks Manor doorbell suddenly began to chime. "Christian would you be a dear and answer the door please?" Lucy called out from her bedroom upstairs.

"Is it Stephen?" he called back from the table in the dining area.

"Of course, dear," her voice carried like song through the house as she responded to her son in kind. "Let the man in."

Christian then quickly scampered up towards the front door whereupon opening from the foyer he was met with the tall, dark and handsome soldier who was dressed in blue denim jeans and a pale pink shirt.

"Hi Christian, you look well," the tall, green-eyed soldier spoke kindly all the while handing the blue-eyed blond a bouquet of freshly bought roses. "These are for your mom. May I come in?"

Christian then nodded his head with an expression of sheer cluelessness for a second before opening his home to the tall and handsome young man. "Come in? I mean, yes, come in. It's cold out tonight."

"Oh, good you're here, you're here," Lucy chuckled as she quickly scurried into the foyer from the top landing of the Sparks Manor staircase. "Dinner is ready. Just need my darling little helpers to assist in serving the meal," she chuckled while playfully landing a giant and gentle tap atop his right arm. "Oh, are the roses for me?" she continued while swiping the bouquet from her smitten young son's hands.

***

157

No more than an hour had passed as the lavish meal of finely grilled sirloin steak, roasted potatoes cooked in goose fat and honey-glazed vegetables was all but served, fed and finished.

"Oh, what a darling you are Stephen Lee Craig," Lucy chuckled as she served up her own batch of homemade salted caramel trifle. "Your parents must be so proud of you. A true warrior you were always destined to become."

"I mean. Yeah I guess," the soldier chuckled as the family all sat together around the candlelit dining table. "I really do miss everyone though. And I'm glad that I came here to see you all before going north of the island to visit my folks."

Christian however just continued to gaze on admirably at his childhood hero as the front doorbell suddenly began to chime.

"I'll get it," the blue-eyed blond muttered as Kenneth sat drowsy from the over intake of good home-cooked food.

And upon opening the forepart door by the foyer, Christian was then met with Sarah and Paul Blossome who both stood in astonishment on the front porch just outside of the house. "Guys, is everything okay?" he quietly asked the siblings.

"No, I'm afraid not," Sarah muttered anxiously. "No one has seen Max since we left him back at the estate, last night."

"Max is gone?" the blue-eyed blond muttered back in dismay. "What about Claire, where is she…?"

"We don't know," Paul whispered all the while Lucy's dinner commenced inside of her homely manor.

"Who is it?" Lucy's voice sang out once again.

Christian then turned his head back towards the inside of the house and called through, "It's just Paul and Sarah."

"Oh, you poor dears, come in, come in out of the cold," she chuckled as she scampered quickly up to the front porch. "Do come in. I'll give you both something nice and warm to eat. Then we'll have Stephen escort you both safely back to your home."

***

And so, another hour had passed after dinner was served, and Lucy had now downed a few glasses of her savoured red rose wine. "These children are my priority, my little booboos. All of them, Stephen dear. My beloved sister, Jane, God rest her soul, would have simply loved to see her two and my own of course, grow into the fine young adults that they are today."

"I'm sure. Now, let's get you to your bed before you have an accident," Stephen chuckled all the while assisting her up off of her seat and into the foyer just beyond the dining area.

"You're such a gentleman, young Stephen Lee Craig. Your father, the war hero, must be so proud," Lucy chuckled and burped as she ascended the stairway up onto the top landing of her pristine and well-kept manor house.

"Sorry about this, Stephen," Naomi explained all the while filling the dirty dishes into the pristine white dishwasher. "She's really taking this vanishing thing literally to heart. I guess the trauma of vanishing loved ones has never truly left her ever since the tragic loss of our father and her sister, way back when in central Africa."

***

Meanwhile in the living room, Christian, Paul, Kenneth, Emma and Sarah all sat together on the two aqua-blue sofas to discuss a plan and execution of such plan.

"This is crazy," Paul grunted in frustration under his breath. "It's almost like, hey let's just allow ourselves to become abducted and hope for the best when we get to the other side."

"Yes, it could work okay. I have the torch, and it has mass effect on him, so as long as I can get it to where he's going, I can use its power to unleash hell upon his face," Kenneth whispered briskly in response.

"Yeah, like that will work out the way that you intend, without him coming for the Artefact at all," Paul chuckled nervously. His tone was dry and sarcastic as they spoke.

"Well, I actually left the Artefact with David earlier this morning," Kenneth argued back.

"LEFT IT WITH DAVID...!" Paul exclaimed rather loudly atop the quiet whispers of their secret meeting. "If David was really our protector, then he wouldn't have allowed that thing of nightmares to touch us in the first place."

"You don't mean that?" Kenneth winced as he saw a hint of resentment fill up within Paul's big brown eyes.

"I never even asked for any of this," Paul muttered as he grabbed hold of his belongings. "None of this would have even happened if you hadn't returned to the Oasis and cursed us all with this goddamn destiny."

And so, just then, all of Lucy's plant pots suddenly ruptured into life as the vast overgrowth of the greenery quickly sprouted around the living room like a wild and messy jungle.

"What was that? What just happened?" Stephen gasped as he and Naomi quickly dashed into that of the now plant-infested living room.

"Mom has green fingers…" Christian responded as he, Emma and Sarah sat idle on the other sofa which was stationed kindly just beside the TV set.

"Interesting?" the tall soldier sighed as he studied the room which Paul had sprouted before inevitably fleeing from the manor.

"Great gardener isn't she…?" Kenneth grinned awkwardly at the confounded tall man.

What are you guys? Stephen pondered as suddenly a strange whooshing sound passed by the house before trembling from an ominous force that mysteriously appeared just outside.

"Four down…" the distinct and unmistakable voice of Prometheus then sounded.

"Oh no, Mom's going to flip," Christian gasped just as the towering sinister shadow of the Titan had overcast itself upon the door of Sparks Manor.

"What was that?" Stephen asked again. "What is going on?"

"Warriors of Piathos, there is no hope left for you now. Do not resist me…" the giant, black-armoured assailant spoke through a raspy tone as he stepped foot in front of the house.

"I am so confused!" Stephen sighed as the humongous Titan towered greatly above height of his own.

"Useless…" Prometheus scoffed as he swiftly and easily tossed Stephen through the banister of the stairs which was stationed at the left side of the foyer.

"Stephen?" Christian exclaimed as he quickly ran passed the bustling Titan to tend to his stunned and wounded friend.

"Time to get cold," Naomi spoke as she swiftly whipped out her glacier-steel sword accompanied by Kenneth who suddenly summoned upon his red and golden-feathered quiver.

And so, suddenly, from within his golden-red quiver, Kenneth pulled from within the pocket a wooden, red bow which illuminated brightly as if it were a bubbling and dazzling lava lamp.

"Sweet…" the Warrior of Fire sighed as he fashioned himself a hot bolt of flaming energy which he launched at Prometheus from his new-found bow.

"Kenneth, watch the house?" Emma exclaimed as she pulled her trident out from its smaller and peaceful state.

"I only need to finish collecting you to complete my transcendence into godhood. And of course, I will need to borrow that Celestial Artefact which you covet most from me," Prometheus chuckled sinisterly all the while commencing into combat with the four Warriors.

Meanwhile, Christian assisted Stephen out onto the front lawn where they could see nothing but greenery for miles and miles.

"Relax. I won't let anybody hurt you," Christian spoke softly. "You know buddy, you were always my hero. And now I have to be yours," he continued while attaching the clear, jewelled bracelet onto his right wrist. "This Artefact helps me to control my powers."

"Your powers…?" Stephen sighed as suddenly Christian's eyes became alive with the spark of electrical discharge.

**

Meanwhile, back inside of the house as Prometheus and the Warriors charged violently into combat, Lucy quickly scampered onto the top of the staircase all the while dressed in her frilly little pink nightgown.

"My beautiful house…!" Lucy exclaimed before keeling over and fainting.

And so, as the fighting continued, Naomi used her glacier-steel sword to defend from the insanely fast attempts of Prometheus' super-sharp whipping strikes.

"Get my mom and everyone else out of here!" Naomi roared as she went toe to toe with the giant and powerful assailant.

"Always the sharp one…" the mysteriously masked villain chuckled as Naomi defended against the blows which he offered painfully upon her.

"No, Naomi," Kenneth muttered as he once again crafted himself another sharp bolt of flaming hot energy. "I am not leaving you to fight him alone."

"How poetic," Prometheus laughed as he again reigned in his glowing purple chains. "The great Warriors of Fire and Ice oppose me well. But no matter, there will be room for you later," he finished before quickly whipping the chain around and snagging Sarah up by her ankles.

"No!" Kenneth cried as he swiftly attempted to grab hold of her hand. But alas he was not fast enough as the black-armoured Titan quickly scooped up the Warrior of the Mind before making a hasty exit and exploding out of the front door.

Chapter 19
The Celestial Dagger of the Circle

"Oh my god, I just got your call," Claire exclaimed as she charged swiftly like the wind into the waiting room of the Angelic Oasis hospital. "He attacked you at your house?" she gasped in sheer horror.

"I don't like the looks of this," Naomi sighed as she spoke to Kenneth, Emma and Claire all the while sitting helplessly within the ER waiting room. "Sarah's gone, Paul's gone and now my little brother too. Mother is going to be so very broken. We have to get everyone back."

"The medics say that Lucy is going to be okay," Emma spoke as she finished talking to the doctors at reception. "Other than psychological and emotional trauma, she's going to be fine. Stephen, on the other hand, is a completely different story. He has sustained some bad nerve damage to his lower spine, and they can't get a proper look at it until the swelling goes down."

"So, what do we do then?" Claire asked as the four teenagers sat helplessly.

"I'll go back to Angel Falls and retrieve the torch," Kenneth said while standing from the hard and plastic seats." You three stick together and protect each other."

"What about you?" Emma inquired as her expression remained troubled.

"Don't worry," he exclaimed. "I'm not going down without a fight." And so, Kenneth left behind the sanctuary of the hospital as he suddenly snuck off into the cold and stormy darkness of the late autumn night.

***

Meanwhile, back at the holding cells, however, Sarah soon found herself waking up within the small and dingy dungeon, along with the five other Warriors which Prometheus had captured. And so, she was also bound to the purple glowing chains that were making it virtually impossible for her to access her telekinetic powers. "Oh, no," she sighed unhappily as she gazed up at her collected ground of friends. "He got me."

"Me too," Christian sighed while feeling lowly without access to his powers. "When this is all said and done, I am so going to shock that badly dressed cosplayer."

"Hey sunshine, you okay?" Paul asked as he slid over beside his sister and Christian.

"Where am I?" she pondered while gazing around with an eye of curiosity. "We need to get out of here... Oh damn, I can't use my powers."

"On the bright side, Sarah, at least we're all here together," Joshua smirked as Eric continued to sit in the silence of the other Piolan Warriors.

"I implore you to tell me why you are so fearless in the face of this matter? And whatever courage has infused you so I'd also like to try it," Sarah asked as she gazed curiously upon the brazen Warrior of Strength.

"Because I know that we're going to escape. Once Claire gets here and out dumbs this super intelligent assailant."

"Oh, dear god," Sarah scoffed sarcastically while rolling her big blue eyes. "Titty power and all that..."

"It makes her feel empowered," Josh chuckled as he stood up from within the small and dingy cell.

"He's right, you know," Max interrupted as he crawled spryly towards the rusted bars of the dingy and damp dungeon. "If there is anyone who can think outside the box, or more importantly outside of this cell, then that person would be in fact my zany, windy and oh so sexy Claire."

***

No more than twenty minutes had passed until Kenneth had arrived at Angel Falls Park, which was empty of walkers due to the overcast and oceanic storm. Despite feeling tired and sweaty from the adrenaline fuelled jog, Kenneth commenced towards the cemetery grounds notwithstanding the fear of Prometheus' uncanny assaults.

"David, this is important..." the Warrior of Fire sighed while expanding the size of his bow and quiver. "Please guide me." And so, as Kenneth stepped foot into the light of the Celestial pocket realm, he soon found himself standing back inside of the warm and brightly lit gardens.

"I know what is happening," David's voice reverbed immensely around the gardens before whisking Kenneth back into the mansion's vast and luxurious lounge room once more. "And yes, you will need this back," he spoke while handing over the stunning golden Artefact.

"David, we're now spread too thin," Kenneth sighed tiredly as he dropped down onto one of the soft and silken armchairs. "We are no match for this guy, Peter or whoever he is."

"Lemonade for you, good sir," Billy muttered as he handed the young Warrior a tall glass of cool and pale fruit juice. "Drink up. You must keep your body cool if your powers are not to falter."

"He's right, Kenneth, drink up," David said as he too sat down on one of the heavenly soft armchairs. "Tonight is the night Kenneth. Tonight, Prometheus will regain his powers and then he will journey into the fiery depths of The Circle of Destiny so that he can barter for his family's return."

"Well that's great confidence building," Kenneth chuckled before swallowing down his tall, cold glass of Billy's homemade lemonade. "So how on Earth do you intend on preventing this from actually happening?"

"There's no need to overthink it," David smiled coyly. "You already have the answer, right there in your hands. Though I advise you to take a different path from the one you used upon coming here," he continued. "I had Billy here search the underground tunnels just below the graveyard. And it appears that the Titan has been lingering around in the ruins below."

And so just then, Kenneth was once again zapped out of the Celestial pocket realm and carried inside of a blinding white light which then returned him to the overcast greenery of the Angelic Oasis burial grounds.

***

Meanwhile, back at the hospital, Naomi, Emma and Claire all waited patiently for Kenneth's return as the lights within the empty waiting room suddenly began to flicker and dim.

"He's here," Claire gasped as suddenly the Titan's eerie shadow slowly crept upon them in the dark…

***

Meantime, however, as Kenneth began to make his way back towards the hospital, he, in actual fact, took the underground tunnels which David had suggested was housing his friends.

And, as he walked a steady pace throughout the dark and dingy tunnels which were illuminated by the flame that he held atop the torch, Kenneth could in fact hear the raspy breath of someone cold and unfriendly slowly stalking upon him.

"All are now mine, except for the two, of fire and ice. I'm hunting for you…"

The ominous cackles of Prometheus could be heard suddenly echoing within the dank stone walls of the tunnels, all the while sending chills shivering right down Kenneth's spine. And so, the Titan's voice commenced to resonate between the dancing light and shadows as he crept.

"Found you," the Titan laughed manically as he suddenly grabbed a firm hold of Kenneth by the throat and tossed him violently into the rocky formation of the man-made tunnels. "Are you ready to join the others? They are so longing to see you again," he taunted while creeping upon the startled young Warrior. "Especially your dear sweet sister, Emma. Oh, she definitely put up one hell of a fight."

Suddenly, becoming infused with rage, Kenneth let out an aggrieved cry of fury as the flames which sat upon the torch began to burn in a stunning haze of pure white light.

"Is that a challenge, Warrior of Fire?" Prometheus chuckled as he and Kenneth swiftly charged towards each other…

166

And with one mighty strike to the head from the Celestial burning torch, Prometheus' helmet was at last shattered and torn from his face...

"No," Kenneth sighed as he gazed wide-eyed upon the assailant which stood in a sudden state of shock before him. "Peter, god I knew it!"

"Don't act so surprised child," the Titan laughed mockingly. "I have lived many lifetimes beyond your entire civilised world. And though I may have walked in step with mankind on this Earth, I did so alone, without my brethren, thanks to that cunning cold hearted Piolan witch, Black. But tonight, all of that will be forever changed."

Kenneth, however, suddenly noticed something very spectacular as he held tightly onto the lantern of Autt within his shaking hands. And from its centre, Kenneth pulled from its core the shining golden blade which also belonged to the Archangel that currently resided within flaming realm of The Circle of Destiny.

"Incredible..." he sighed all the while hypnotically studying the ancient and magnificent Artefact.

"Ah," Prometheus sighed as he stared down upon the Celestial blade with glistening eyes of hopeless longing. "Oh, sublime one, how long I have waited. And now with the curse removed from that wretched haunted house, I can finally travel to the Circle and barter for my family's freedom," the Titan spoke as he sobbed happily through misty eyes of sheer and pure joy.

***

Meanwhile, back at the now cramped dark and dingy dungeon, Claire Stevenson's cries for help could in fact be heard resonating in wailing song from within the long and winding underground tunnels.

"Waa-aa-aa-aa-aa-aa-aa-aa-aa-aa-ah...! I'm going mad in here! Eee-ee-ee-ee-eh! Oo-oo-oo-oo-oo-oh! Aaa-aa-aa-aa-aa-aa-aa-aa-aah! Loopy, loopy, loopy, loopy...!" Claire yelled as she squeezed her face through the bars of the cell in a pathetic attempt to escape.

"I thought you said she'd be the one to get us out of here?" Sarah asked as a confounded expression painted itself across her face.

"Oh my god, babe you are killing me!" Max laughed insanely hard that his sides were beginning to hurt as Claire continued to call out and sing for help.

"Oh no, face stuck, I bit my tongue… Ouch, guys face stuck? Hell-oo-oo-oo-oo…?" she continued to call and shout out. "Titan guy, could you come and help me?"

Then suddenly, Prometheus had returned to the cell with a bludgeoned and chained up Kenneth Feather in hand. "Don't look so surprised children," he spoke as the seven other Warriors minus Claire however, all gazed up at him with expressions of sheer dismay and true sickening horror. "This is merely just another lesson in history for me to teach you."

"Mr McKenzie…?" Eric gasped all the while gazing upon his old teacher with wide eyes of disbelief.

And just as Peter McKenzie hurtled Kenneth into the dingy and damp holding cell, he rolled his eyes at Claire who was squished between the rusting old dungeons bars before pushing her back to sit with the others.

"Where's the torch?" Josh asked as the group quickly rallied around the wounded Warrior.

"He took the blade," Kenneth winced as the blood from his wound stained the pale skin of his face. "What are we going to do?"

"Ah, yes it worked," Claire chuckled victoriously all the while holding the golden Artefact in hand. "Don't know what it is but, yes Ha-ha!"

"You have it?" Kenneth gasped as he jumped forward in disbelief. "How did you get it?"

"Oh, it's very simple you see," Claire began to speak as she handed over the Artefact to Kenneth. "Just make a big and wonderful decoy and then seize the opportunity as it passes."

"Titty power and all," Emma chuckled as she shook her head in surprise. "You, Claire Stevenson, never change who you are."

Bound in chains with one and other, the remaining nine Warriors of Piathos all waited patiently together as Prometheus set off to retrieve the last of them which was frosty Queen of ice herself.

***

Meanwhile as Naomi ran through the cold and rainy streets of the Angelic Oasis at night, she began to feel the cold and ungodly presence of someone uncanny stalking and creeping upon her in the darkness. Her long, dark hair stuck fast to her face as her ponytail whipped back and forth within the oceanic winds of the passing storm.

"You cannot hide from me forever, Naomi," Prometheus called out as he stalked her through the streets of the west coast side of town. "I can sense your filthy Piolan-infused powers, and I am coming for you. You are the hunted," he continued to taunt all the while sneaking into the woodland between the west coast and the park.

Undefined to the Titan as he crept through the woodland however, Naomi Sparks impressively snuck above and beyond the history teacher's gaze as she, in actual fact, stationed herself atop the shadows and amongst the tree tops with her glacier-steel sword in hand.

"I can sense your powers," he exclaimed while searching the rainy path of the woodland walkway.

"Can you sense this?" Naomi grunted as she leaped down upon him while freezing over her sword and slicing it across the mad assailant's face.

"Argh!" he exclaimed in anger as the red blood of his weakened state quickly began to pour out freely from his newly placed battle scar. "Always the sharp one, aren't you, Naomi Sparks?"

"Cold as ice," she grunted back in anger as the newly exposed Peter pulled from his back, the purple glowing chains of magical binding.

"Oh, I have been so longing…" he began while suddenly whipping up the last Warrior within his mystical bindings, "to melt that frosty grin off your face…"

***

Shortly thereafter however, back at the dungeons, Prometheus had returned to his underground layer with the last and fiercest Warrior firmly in hand.

"Get in there and be quiet!" he roared while chucking icy teenager into the cell beside the others. "Now that you have all arrived, it is at last time to perform the ritual in which I will use your collective powers to return me of my own."

The tall, dark and ominous villain then turned to a small wooden table which sat merely but a few feet away from the dingy, old holding cell. And so, he swiftly twirled away from the Warriors' gazes as he commenced onwards to prepare a dark and shady spell.

"For many years, I have scoured the Earth and Witching realms in search of the most useful and powerful Artefacts," he spoke giddily in anticipation of his soon to be coming.

"This little trinket that I have here in my hand is in fact an amulet ring, which once belonged to a witch from the Scottish Kingdom of Soleray Valley. It will in actual fact bind me to the magics which have blessed you with your abnormal augmented gifts," he giggled joyfully while producing the small and ruby-red gem to that of the onlooking Warriors.

The manically giddy Titan produced a very old and worn-out scroll which he excitedly opened with a gleaming wide glance of anticipation. "This is, in actual fact, a parchment which is dusted with magical properties. It allows any user of man's world to perform but one act of magic. I had received this scroll from the Norwegian Witching Kingdome of Lightwey Valley."

And lastly, he turned his searing gaze towards that of the Warriors of Piathos while giving them an arrogant and sinister grin, "And, of course, I had received these mystical binding chains, my armour and my cloak from the American witches of Whitevale Valley. And now that I have everything that I need, it is time for me to once again dawn the glory of my former self..."

The Warriors of Piathos sat idle as the Titan powdered the group with the dust from the scroll before locking the ruby ring onto that of his left index finger.

'O' ancients magics of the past, hear me now. Celuni lio morbos don fort, magiria impenitri, impiria, spirixo. Return me to my former self.'

The trembling Titan chanted whilst the ruby-red gem on his hand suddenly became aglow with light as the energy which bound the Warriors from their powers, suddenly began to fade away and with it the magnetic aura which infused them with their amazing and blessed gifts.

And so just then, Prometheus was at last free of his half mortal coil and was once again remade in the image of his former self. "Yes, yes, yes…" he cried in sheer joy all the while creating a searing hot ball of magma and flames between the palms of his godly hands. "Do not fret, children. You see, unlike mine your powers cannot be taken. They will regenerate within your cells very soon."

"Now what do you intend on doing with us?" Kenneth asked as the mad assailant quelled the hot blazing ball with the sheer force of his very own thoughts and willpower.

"I'd like to say that I want to kill you all right here and right now," Prometheus chuckled, as he trembled from the overwhelming joy of his triumphant victory. "But that would be far too easy. I want you all to witness the rise of a new era under my great rule. And when my family returns, we shall once again become the great Kings who once used to rule triumphantly over all others…"

And with that being said, Prometheus turned away from the Warriors of Piathos and fled swiftly off into the shadows of the cold and unkind underground tunnels.

Chapter 20
Return to the Dreaded Hell House

"How on Earth do we escape now?" Sarah exclaimed as she rattled the chains which no longer glowed with magic. "I don't have my tiara with me and I can't think clearly."

"Hold on," Kenneth sighed before taking the Celestial blade from behind his back and then striking it into the null and void chains. And then, suddenly, from the instant that he attacked the now dim and grey chains, the bland mental bindings which confined the ten Warriors together suddenly broke away and fell to the ground in a cloud of black dust and debris.

"Okay, now we need to get out of this cell before he notices that the blade is missing," Josh said as he attempted to kick open the door. "Damn, my powers are still low."

"Step aside," Kenneth sighed while again using the Celestial blade to cut open the bars of the dimly lit dungeon chamber…

**

No more than a few minutes had passed before the group soon found themselves standing amidst the tombs of the Oasis cemetery once again.

"Quickly Warriors," Billy's voice sounded as the teens all clamoured close together just beyond the Celestial gateway. "Come this way. David has successfully retrieved the missing Artefacts of both Sarah and Paul."

"Billy, what, how…?" Sarah pondered as the little old man quickly guided the teenagers away from the dangers of the outside world.

And so, just then, the Warriors of Piathos soon found themselves once again standing within the great halls of David's Celestial mansion.

"I can see that you found the true prize," David spoke as he swiftly handed the teenagers warm food, cold water and a fresh pair of clean clothes. "You are not safe on the outside, not without the Dagger of the Circle in your possession."

"David, thank you so much," Kenneth sighed as he and the other Warriors quickly indulged in the meal which Billy had prepared in anticipation of their arrival.

"You're welcome," David smiled softly. "Now eat, you must recharge in order to regain the strength of your powers. It will not be long before I send you all off to the entrance of Autt's hidden dimension."

***

Sometime later after refreshing and recharging with their clean clothes and hot meals, the ten young Warriors of Piathos soon rounded up together within the armoury of David's Celestial mansion.

"The place to which you are all about to journey is the most dangerous and perilous one," David spoke as he stood tall in hand with his humongous glowing white trident. "I need you all to trust in yourselves and in one another."

He continued as Paul passed Kenneth a friendly and apologetic nod which the Fire Warrior returned to him in kind.

"Trust in the power which has been bestowed upon you," he commenced. "And trust in the Divine Artefacts of both Celestial and Mystical properties. The more attached that you become with these objects and with each other, the more secure in these powers your connection will become…"

And finally, as David smiled proudly upon them, he commenced to wave his trident above his head, filling the room with the brightest of Celestial light all the while transporting the Warriors to the entrance of the haunting and dreaded old Hell House.

Chapter 21
Into Autt's Realm

"One night later and we're standing right back here again," Naomi chuckled sarcastically as she and the group commenced forward into the dark and dingy old manor, lit only by Kenneth's pyrokinetic power.

As the Warriors travelled down together into the basement with their Artefacts in hand, they suddenly happened upon the old sarcophagus which had recently become breached.

"This is it," Christian sighed as he gazed into the open coffin to see a glowing-blue pool of glistening and otherworldly water. "Hey Emma, you up for a swim...?"

"Let's go," the redheaded girl responded as she linked hands with Sarah and Claire before jumping simultaneously into the pool which sounded like the ocean waves crashing calmly upon the Bay Shore.

"Safe enough," Paul muttered nervously as he too lunged into the blue waters of the glistening otherworld.

And so, one by one, the other Warriors of Piathos quickly hopped into the calm and swirling waters of the sarcophagus as they soon travelled from their Earthly plane to that of the fiery and red world of Autt's Celestial dimension.

"Oh my god," Joshua sighed in wonder as he gazed out longingly at the burning red world which dazzled like an alien planet all around him. All the while strange and magnetic boulders flittered and drifted by as if they were nothing more than that of sweet and harmless bubbles. "Did we just land on Mars?"

"Oh, we're not on Mars silly," Claire chuckled at her curly-haired cousin. "We're in some far, far away land that no one has ever heard of before."

Kenneth then giggled lightly at Claire's comment before turning around to gaze upon a tall and mighty volcano which sat proudly atop an amber canyon as it spread out with great growth of otherworldly volcanic bushes and giant, red petal plants that were breathing cool burst of air vastly before them. "This is it," he sighed nervously in the face of the dry and storming blood-red skies. "The Circle of Destiny…"

"Looks like there's a safe path just up ahead," Eric spoke as he pointed out a long and winding walkway overhead. "That trail seems to be leading safely up the face of the mountain." And as Eric's voice echoed out across the canyon valley, hot flames and molten lava violently burst into the air before cooling into the floating magnetic rocks which then drifted on by. "Perfectly safe…?" he smiled anxiously.

"Come on," Sarah spoke as she commenced to walk forward along the burning amber canyon. "The longer we wait the more likely it will be that Mr McKenzie will reach Autt and barter for his wish."

"She's right," Kenneth sighed in response. "Let's go."

***

And so, sometime later, the Warriors had stumbled upon an underground cave which was illuminated by a row of the same cone lanterns which had housed the infamous blade of the Archangel, Autt, himself.

"Is it empty?" Claire asked as the team progressed further into the warmly lit cavern.

And as they continued on into the vast expanding stairwell, Kenneth felt a strange and pulling sensation as the blade suddenly began to tremble from within his belt. He felt it to be something odd while removing the Artefact from his side. "Whoa, no kidding when David said that Artefacts actually become bonded to their owners."

And so, finally upon approaching the top of the swerving and swirling stairwell, the Warriors of Piathos were then met with a strange glacier and crystal barricade which sheltered that of a giant and ancient fortress.

How on earth do we get through this? Paul wondered as the fire and lava spewed angrily in the distance behind them.

Kenneth lifted the Celestial blade as it continued to tremble and shake in his hand. "I'm getting the feeling that I should use the Dagger of the Circle again."

"Yeah, yeah, yeah…!" Claire exclaimed excitedly as she gazed on wide-eyed with anticipation. "Just like the purple chains and the bars to the dungeon cell."

Taking a brief moment to breath however as he pondered. Kenneth then struck the vibrating blade swiftly into the solid hind of the stunning glacier and crystallised wall.

And so, just then, a wild and strong windy vacuum suddenly gusted outward from the abruptly punctured wall. As it fractured widely open, the insanely powerful suction then dragged the Warriors aggressively into its grasp before closing over like a giant formation of solid ice.

"Where's Emma?" Kenneth panicked suddenly as he and the others frantically glanced at the red stone citadel around them.

"I'm out here!" her voice sounded from the other side of the giant glacier wall. "The blast knocked me backward before pulling you all in."

Kenneth shook his head and grimaced in confusion. "How…?" he asked.

"It doesn't matter," she called back. "I can find an alternative route."

"Emma, don't you dare…" Kenneth exclaimed with his big brother tone. But to his surprise, Emma had already turned away and taken off to the side of the mountain.

"Kenneth, we should press on," Eric spoke as he attempted to pull at his friend's left arm. "And guys, I am sorry for giving up earlier. Josh you're right, I don't just skate to win. I skate because it is within my blood, just like our powers. So let's use these powers to save the goddamn world."

***

And so, as the Warriors travelled further into the city of fire, the heat from the surrounding volcano was slowly starting to become all the more potent and formidably intense as they commenced into that of a giant and black-stoned castle.

"God, it's so hot. I think that I might be getting a suntan…" Claire panted as she guzzled down an entire litre of cool bottled water.

"I'm definitely getting sunburned guys," Christian panted as he too guzzled down a nice cool drink. "My little arms are hot and my cute little face is beat going red…"

"Max, I'm so hot. Here, feel my chest," Claire huffed and puffed as she dragged herself on tiredly just behind her boyfriend.

Max gazed upon her sweaty and clammy face and smiled lovingly as he chuckled, "You are so hot no matter what. Now, back to climbing this oven, shall we?"

***

Meanwhile, on the outside of the city, Emma had suddenly begun to climb up the hovering boulders as they were carried adrift like a flurry of solid black clouds of sheer rocky iron.

"Damn, why does being a redhead have to suck right now?" she panted through the intense heat of the amber and red Celestial world.

Leaping from stone to stone, Emma attempted to use her powers of hydrokinesis to soften and cool some of the more unstable rocks as they wilted away like ash upon her touch. Nonetheless, her powers only excelled vapours of hot mist and steam instead of cool bodies of lavish and heavy waters.

"God damn it. That's hot!" she exclaimed while using her gymnastic skills to vault across the open crevasses with her glowing-blue trident in hand.

And so, as she continued to scale along the unstable summit on the outside, Kenneth and the other Warriors suddenly found themselves at a halt as they travelled further into the recesses of the ancient and black stone castle.

"Dead end Kenneth," Naomi stated as she and the others gazed down at a huge pool of bubbling hot lava which was cooking overtime in the huge crater that was stationed between two vast chambers of a broken staircase.

Paul gazed around at the ancient black castle looking for an alternative way to travel safely across. "There's no way up there," he called out all the while pointing towards the ledge that hung just above the boiling crater.

"No kidding? How do we get up there then?" Josh asked as he studied the unstable rocky formation. "That looks like it might cave in, Paul. I'm wondering why you are not overthinking this right now?"

"Oh, believe me," Paul chuckled nervously. "I am overthinking it."

Kenneth, however, pondered himself for a second as he suddenly remembered something before turning around to look at Sarah. "Teleport, you can teleport…"

"What?" the blue-eyed blonde gasped. "I only managed it that one time…" she replied as Kenneth took hold of her hands.

"I know," he responded softly. "But you willed yourself to be closer to me."

And so, just then, Kenneth and Sarah commenced forth with their first kiss together as the magnetic rocks just continued to hover on in the sky above them.

"Hey, that's my sister!" Paul exclaimed as he grimaced in disgust.

"Now, Sarah. Will yourself up there. Will it like you willed yourself into the Hell House when you came to find me on Halloween, last night," Kenneth whispered to her softly.

Sarah then glanced up towards the upper ledge and pondered to herself as she suddenly began to will her mind into moving her body through the fabrics of matter and space.

And so, just then, her clear-jewelled tiara once again became aglow with the gleam pink light as she suddenly vanished from sight, setting off another shocking rupture of matter in her wake.

"Oh my god it worked," Sarah chuckled as she found herself standing atop the balcony which lead further up into the castle.

"Sarah, what do you see…?" Paul's voice sounded out from afar.

"I see the exit, a loose chunk of floor against the wall and lots of empty plant pots," she called back.

"Is there anything up there that could get us all across?" Naomi then abruptly yelled up.

"Yes, I have an idea…" Sarah shouted back as she used her telekinesis to carry the huge slab of rock which sat firmly against the wall behind her. And so, she began to transfer the heavy object with great strain and removed it away from the balcony above overhead.

And then, all of a sudden, the Warriors of Piathos were all at once amazed when Sarah Blossome impressively carried down the ginormous slab of rock before holding it carefully atop the stewing crevasse amidst the broken staircase.

"I can't hold on!" Sarah exclaimed while grimacing from the strain. "A little help here please…?"

"Hang on sis," Paul spoke as he reached out to the alien-like overgrowth which sat amidst the castles stony interior and commanded it to hold the slab down securely in place.

"Nice, good work guys," Kenneth smiled as he and the other Warriors safely travelled across the newly made staircase and up onto the balcony where Sarah had now tiredly awaited for their arrival.

***

Meanwhile, back on the outside of the mountain however, Emma was still commencing to climb and scale along the side of the rocky summit as she swiftly leaped and bound from boulder to boulder.

"This feels like some crazy ass assault course!" she yelled to herself while lunging across several open paths and landing upon ashy slopes with a tremendous amount of great and sheer force.

Gazing upwards at the dry and stormy sky, however, Emma could see that so many of the larger rocks and boulders simply remained stationed in a firm stance of magnetic equilibrium.

"Okay, just this last outreach and we're on the homerun," she panted to herself before using her trident to force motion into some of the rocks as they glided peacefully amidst the top of the mountain's ridge.

***

Meanwhile, Kenneth and the others finally made it to the top but were all once again halted by another obstacle that sat plainly within their path. "You've got to be kidding me?" Christian wept as the Warriors were now faced with a giant fort which was bridged between the castle and the temple atop the very mouth of the angry volcano.

"Why is it raining rocks and lava?" Claire sarcastically scoffed as the Warriors all studied the deadly crossing which sat scalding between them and their target.

"How do we get through here?" Eric pondered as he rattled his brain for a more solid answer. "This blows!" he grunted as a sudden realisation switched on like a night light within his mind.

"What's with the happy face Eric, something smart crossed your mind?" Josh asked as he gazed on at his slim, Japanese-American friend with an expression of sheer curiosity.

"Naomi and Claire, together, they could theoretically cause a blizzard," Eric spoke sharply as the wheels of wonder turned around in his head. "Just like David said. We have to trust in each other as well as trusting ourselves."

"Okay," Claire exclaimed excitedly as she took hold of Naomi's right hand.

"Wait," Max suddenly interrupted. "If we expose an active volcano to a sudden burst of cold, it would indefinitely cause an eruption and destroy this entire castle."

"I wasn't finished," Eric swiftly commenced. "Kenneth has the power of pyrokinesis. He can, in theory, create a safe space around us while the girls here keep said space cool."

Naomi then rolled her big brown eyes as she once again took hold of Claire's left hand. "Why not…"

And so, Kenneth turned his gaze towards that of Sarah and smiled at her before commencing forth onto the battlefield of heat with both of his arms firmly stretched out. "I'm not going to be able to divert these flames forever guys. Whatever you're going to do, you better do it fast."

And so, just then, both Claire and Naomi suddenly began to focus on the molecules that were swimming around them as they, in turn, swiftly began to stir the waves of wind and cold to their will.

"Run!" Josh exclaimed as all together, the Warriors of Piathos suddenly made a swift dash within the sphere of safety as they collectively moved in a unit from one end of the fort to the next.

And, as the large creaking doors to the grand, red stone temple suddenly opened up for the Warriors as they travelled, instantly lit from the corridor within was a row of Autt's lanterns that were lined up against the interior of the walls from inside of the godly and otherworldly fortress.

Kenneth and the other Warriors however casually stepped foot into the grandeur and ominous tower as the raging lava pit hissed and roared in anger behind them.

And with the doors closing firmly behind them, the Piolan Warriors saw that this part of the temple was, in actual fact, not sitting in ruin but was actually designed in scale with a similarity to that of David's Celestial mansion, albeit the colour pallet was far harsher in tone.

"What's going on here?" Sarah asked when suddenly the heating pressure mysteriously rifted away and in its place was a very cool and calming fresh breeze.

Just then, however, out of the walls of the temple and from one of the Archangel paintings, which sat above the row of lanterns, stepped out suddenly a huge and mighty figure with a giant set of six wings which were spanning out at a grand scale of sixteen inches on each end.

The Warriors of Piathos had all then realised just who exactly was standing before them.

"I am Autt, keeper to The Circle of Destiny… How did you, mere humans come upon this place?" he asked as the Warriors rounded closer to each other. "Speak," he continued to ask all the while pulling an impressively large and golden Arcane sword from the sash of his belt.

Autt however towered incredibly over and above the nine Warriors approximately twelve feet tall. And his stunning, golden-forged armour also reflected that of the oceans deep. Along with his lengthy, strawberry hair and beard which floated gracefully beside him, he was most certainly not an image to be trifled with.

Kenneth Feather however then decided to step forward as he swiftly produced the shuddering dagger which truly belonged to the Archangel himself. "Does this belong to you?"

"Where did you get that?" the mighty Celestial Being inquired. "Are you the sublime one?"

"We are the Warriors of Piathos, creations of the Oracles from that far off and distant world," Kenneth calmly began to explain.

"Although, we are simply human of course, born and bred on that blue planet Earth. Another Celestial Being led us here so that we could return you this dagger in the hopes to keep it out of the hands of Prometheus and to stop him from bartering this with you for his wish."

Glancing down at his blade, Autt sheathed away his stunning, golden sword before proceeding onward to speak as he welcomed the Warriors to walk alongside him.

"I have not seen this dagger in many millennia," he suddenly began to speak as they strolled. "It was taken from me by a very powerful force of magic, the Oracle, known by The Nothing as Black Poison but better known to everyone else by her real name, Black, the Piolan Oracle of night…"

Admiring his own craftsmanship however, Autt let out a prolonged and solemn sigh as he suddenly returned the Celestial blade back into that of Kenneth Feather's hands.

"What's this for?" Kenneth asked as he gazed up at the Archangel with eyes of curiosity.

"Through these doors within my throne room chambers, the Titan does sit," Autt began as he pointed over towards a large golden and black chamber which sat at the end of the Celestial hallways.

"He now awaits my presence to barter anything that he can so that the Circle may give him the power in releasing his kin from their capture. After losing them so tragically inside of a prison, that was so masterfully crafted by the Piolan Oracle's magic. Go forth sublime one, your destiny awaits. I however shall remain out here with your peers until their presence is further required."

"Me?" Kenneth implored with a sudden yelp of panic. "I can't just go in there alone."

"Once your deed within the chamber is fulfilled, you must then return my blade to me," Autt's voice echoed as the last entrance before the Warriors suddenly began to move open…

"Hello, Kenneth Feather. I knew you'd come here, sublime one," Prometheus spoke as he stood facing towards a giant fall of pouring lava.

Pulling the dagger free from his belt again, Kenneth cautiously approached the Titan as he commenced forth to talk. "Peter, this can't go on the way that you want."

"Yes Kenneth, please let us discuss? What we could do together if you joined me 'o sublime one," the Titan spoke as he slowly turned around to meet faces with the young Piolan Warrior.

"Please, for every time that I have heard people call me this sublime one, I slowly begin to ponder upon the meaning. And it makes me wonder about my recurring dream and about my ruby-red eye and this mysterious goddess Red that no one is willing to tell me about," Kenneth exclaimed as he and the Titan slowly began to walk in circles of each other.

"I know," Prometheus muttered softly to Kenneth as he showed a genuine expression of concern upon his face. "But together we can unearth the secrets which your heart desires most."

"Nah," Kenneth chuckled sarcastically in response. "I think I'll ponder on it for just a little while longer."

"We could be great together, Kenneth. You are more than just any simple chosen Warrior. You are, in actual fact, born of the heavens. And from the moment that you stepped foot onto the Oasis, I knew that I was standing in the presence of a miracle... A legend if I do say so myself."

***

And so, just then, from the outside of the temple and right above the chamber's peak, Emma had finally arrived upon the fortress which housed the world's deities within that of Autt's inner Circle of Destiny.

And as she stepped swiftly along the red stone rooftops, Emma had, in fact, begun to overhear the conversation which was occurring between her big brother and the insanely powerful Titan within the grand chamber beneath her very feet.

"No!" she gasped in horror, while searching the temple's rooftop for an entrance into the chamber below. "Aha!" Emma sighed, as she suddenly spotted an open hatch atop the pristine and red stone tower.

And so, just then, Emma suddenly began to strike the spearheads of her trident into the crack of the rooftop trying exceedingly hard to summon upon a body of water.

"Come on, come on," she exclaimed over and over, all the while striking hard and fast upon the opened hatch which was bleeding that of an amber glow of bright, warm light. "Come on, come on, I need water…"

Just then, suddenly, from her glowing-blue trident, came that of a hot and hydrokinetic pulse of boiling water which tore apart the hatch beneath her feet.

"What?" Prometheus yelped in anger, as he turned around to see Emma, as she swiftly fell through the ceiling amongst a column of water. "Why, you little, do not interfere with your brother's destiny, sublime o' child of Andreas," the now infuriated Titan roared, as he formed between his hands a ball of searing hot and molten lava.

And, just as Prometheus swiftly turned around to strike his fury upon Emma, Kenneth had crafted another sharp bolt of flaming hot energy before striking it into the back of the unsuspecting Titan.

Roaring in agony, Prometheus removed the burning hot bolt before crushing into dust, as if it were nothing more than a measly twig. "This is not how I envisioned our final meeting to be. But I suppose that killing two sublime children will have to be a sacrifice that I make, for the good of my fallen brethren… A shame really, together we could have ruled the world."

But before Prometheus could lift the searing hot ball of magma, he was suddenly shrouded amidst a swirling flurry of Eric Tony's white mist. And, as the dancing cloud made contact with giant, black-armoured assailant, he instantly froze stiff within its stasis, all the while the remaining Warriors quickly entered inside of the throne room chamber.

Emma, however, suddenly and quickly made pursuit towards her older brother and that of the others as they finally regrouped together just before the open falls of pouring lava.

Then, all of a sudden, the mist which paralysed Prometheus onto one spot quickly ignited in flame before exploding outward in a violent plume of deadly hot and burning eruptions.

Prometheus then angrily rose from the ground and roared at the Warriors like a wild beast as he, suddenly, glared over at Kenneth who still had the Dagger of the Circle firmly in hand.

"The blade…!" the Titan barked, but before he could muster the power in creating another hot ball of searing hot lava, Christian, then, quickly struck him down with a sudden bolt of supercharged thunderous lightning.

"I am going to kill you all," he muttered while forming between his hands a brightly burning sphere of sizzling hot magma…

The Warriors all then gathered together and readied themselves for defence against the Titan's insanely and powerful attack.

Prometheus grinned menacingly at the group as he quickly began to gather between his hands an immensely large amount of great and volcanic power.

"Goodbye, Warriors of Piathos," he smiled with an expression of victory.

Max instinctively held up both of his hands and in an unexpected moment, he suddenly began to cry out…

'Shield!'

And so, just then, from within his gauntlets, Max suddenly began to craft around himself and the other Warriors an impressive layer of glistening and silvery energy which quickly sheltered the teenagers from an imminent and painful death. Looking surprised by his sudden creation, Max lowered down his hands and in turn lowered the molecular shield which glistened around them.

Suddenly, charging once again, Kenneth and Prometheus clashed violently into each other, and with one fatal strike, Kenneth plunged the Dagger of the Circle savagely into the Titan's heart before falling simultaneously into the burning abyss below.

And, as they both fell, Prometheus gave a coy smile while whispering softly into the Piolan Warrior's ear. "And so the student surpasses the teacher…"

"No!" Sarah and Emma both screamed as the Warriors suddenly rallied around the hole in the ground which bubbled away with a river of hot and molten lava.

And just then, from inside the flaming pit of burning death, the Dagger of the Circle suddenly went flying out of the fiery abyss before landing on the ground just behind Emma and the others.

"Can someone give me a hand…?" Kenneth's voice suddenly sounded from the scalding pit below.

And so, Emma's heart suddenly skipped a beat upon hearing her brother's cry for help as she was washed over by the sudden wave of miraculous relief.

"Guys, hello, are you there? It's really hot down here…" he called out once again, as Joshua Stevenson began to climb down into the burning crevasses with his super strength to retrieve Kenneth and bring him back up to the surface.

"Oh, Kenneth thank god you're alive. I thought that you were dead!" Emma sighed joyfully, as she and the others simultaneously lunged forth to embrace the Warrior of Fire with a singular group hug.

"What, me, nah, I'm way too busy to die," he coughed and spurted from the inhalation of volcanic smoke. "I've got a lot on my mind with my red-ruby eye, the sublime one and all the rest of that."

***

Feeling a great sense of relief however, the entire squadron of magically augmented teenagers then returned the Celestial Artefact back into the hands of its once and rightful owner, the Archangel Autt, of the mystical and fiery realm, The Circle of Destiny.

With the Artefact safely returned to its rightful home, the Warriors of Piathos journeyed back into their realm and away from the burning alien world, The Circle of Destiny.

And so, upon leaving the haunted Hell House behind, which sat dejectedly at the peak of the abandoned road, at the break of dawn, the tired group of ten teenagers all returned safely into the arms of their loved ones at their homes that resided within the pristine and warmly welcoming island of the Angelic Oasis…

Chapter 22
Something Recalled

Sunday, November 2, 2008. Angelic Oasis.
After fabricating a story which the teenagers soon told every one of their maniacal and suicidal teacher had all but died down. Life amongst the people on the Oasis once again became that of the steady and solemn solace to which it once and always was.

And as Kenneth once again slipped off gently into the memory of his unclear mind at the dead of night, he was then returned into a nightmare which tortured his very mind and soul, as he slept within the bedroom at the back of Sparks Manor.

Kenneth stood frantic and frozen in fear, on the peak of a foreign mountain, as a huge and ungodly hurricane stormed violently overhead. He was only a child at the time, not much older than six. And as the storm raged on angrily overhead, the young Kenneth could see what appeared to be a strange woman dressed in the most tranquil of heavenly white silk.

And as Kenneth peered ever closer to the perfection of the woman's image, he could see that the redheaded stranger was in fact unscathed by the chaos which whirled around her.

Then suddenly, Kenneth could hear the faint cry of a long lost yet familiar voice calling out to the blurred images that scurried frantically around him

"The Artefact!"

Kenneth looked up again and saw that the serene woman was holding in her hands a pristine, red-jewelled amulet which she began to use in summoning the violent tempest from the cosmos above and beyond.

188

And as Kenneth gazed on, he could see that the woman had grabbed hold of a man by the scruff of his neck. He was someone that Kenneth could not make out clearly, however, through the indistinct haze of his dreamy memory.

"Jane!"

The familiar voice echoed out once again. And then the sudden realisation of the name, Jane, quickly startled the young boy into an adrenaline-fuelled charge, to which he sharply called out ...

"Mommy..."

Suddenly, Kenneth crashed violently into the woman as she tarried atop the mountain edge, which then caused the ruby-red jewel amulet to subsequently shatter all over his face upon impact...

"I got you son, I got you..."

The sound of a familiar yet unclear voice spoke indistinctly as Kenneth was suddenly jolted...

Awake.

Gazing around at the inside of his bedroom however, Kenneth could only see that of his little cousin as he continued to snore peacefully in the next bed beside him. And all the while Christian snoozed blissfully, Kenneth's mind suddenly started to rumble and race as many and more questions swiftly began to occur.

"Who are you...?" Kenneth then sighed in whispers to himself, as he once again lay down and pondered deeply into the jungle of his darkened and mystified mind dreams.